Millie's
Christmas
Spirit

Millie's Christmas Spirit

Tina Peterson Scott

Foutz Fables & More Mesa, AZ

ISBN: 978-0-9891581-6-9

Published by:
Foutz Fables & More
Mesa, Arizona

Cover design by Tina Scott © by Foutz Fables & More

Printed in the United States of America

Dedication

To my husband and my children. Always.

A special thanks to Betsy, Niki, and Cheryl for their encouragement and help, to Valerie Ipson and Joyce DiPastena for their thoughtful critiques, and to Joyce Horstman for her excellent editing skills.

"To be yourself in a world that is constantly trying to make you something else is the greatest accomplishment."
Ralph Waldo Emerson

One

Millie Crump pulled off the highway east of Solomon, Arizona, the hair on her arms rising in apprehension. She stared at the abandoned Ballard Hotel with its surrounding twenty-four acres of unmanicured desert. Hopefully, this year she would overcome both ghosts from her Christmases past.

She groaned and gripped the steering wheel.

How does one explain a relationship with a ghost who haunts at Christmastime, her empathy for his grieving soul, or her desire to help him pass on? She no longer understood it herself. Lonny Medina had been there through it all, and together they'd done everything in their power to rescue their ghost, but it hadn't been enough.

Fourteen years ago, her father had abandoned them, and Mama had dragged her away to start a new life in Phoenix. She never saw Lonny again. Or the Christmas ghost

Her phone chimed, and recognizing the number, Millie answered, listened with a frown, and then responded, "Mr. Rumley, I have no intention of moving back here. How might I ease your worry in that regard?" Her boss had already called her twice and she had barely arrived. She added a touch of sweetness to her voice, hoping to avoid being fired while completing her hidden agenda. "Back by Monday? Today is Friday and I'm not sure if I can get anyone to work here over the weekend." Yes, she could have accomplished her agenda, or rather her company's agenda, by phone. Yes, she realized her importance to the Phoenix team. And yes, she knew this was an important account. How many times did he need to tell her?

Millie eased her car forward. When she did, the call dropped. She looked at her phone to make sure, smiled, and continued down the unpaved circle drive of the Ballard Hotel, nerves tingling in her stomach. Though rescuing the ghost of Emerson Ballard was her ultimate goal, her mind wandered to Lonny Medina. Although she shouldn't have expected him to come after her fourteen years ago, she had. Fourteen years was plenty of time to get over someone, but now that she was back, the old feelings of abandonment by her first and only love revived.

Millie took a deep, sighing breath. It would not be good to cry over Lonny. She had done enough of that. This was a short visit. The property would officially be sold in ten days, the hotel destroyed not long after. She squared her shoulders. No, she would not allow herself regrets over unkept promises. This was her time to shine—to flaunt her success under the noses of the locals and to gain Emerson Ballard his eternal rest before the buyers ripped his home apart.

"Why isn't Lonny here yet?" With a leaden feeling in the pit of her stomach, Millie drummed her nail extensions on the steering wheel of her sporty red Mazda Miata, an indisputable symbol of her success; growing up in Solomon, Millie couldn't afford a car, let alone acrylic nails, eyelash extensions, dermabrasions, or her three-hundred-dollar color weave. Life here had been real—a little too real at times—and she preferred having food on her table.

Almost instinctively, she rolled down her window, tenderly touching the leaves of the now-mature mesquite tree near the front entrance, the musky-sweet desert smell wafting into her car. As children, she and Lonny had climbed the thorn-riddled sapling, its rough bark tearing their pants. The thorns had cut their hands and legs, and Millie had received a whipping for her wounds. Back then, Lonny had been her lifeline to normalcy and hope in an increasingly volatile homelife. She blinked back the memories. Her childish reminiscing served no good purpose.

Millie stepped from her Miata and tugged at her pencil skirt. A wave of nostalgia hit her with the crunch of gravel on the hard earth beneath her designer heels. Bats dove for insects and the late afternoon sun nodded toward the horizon, casting long shadows across the sparse Chihuahuan Desert. When a large bat dipped toward her, Millie raced to the hotel, her heart jolting in her chest. Then she stood on the front step and chuckled. She really had become a city girl.

Chips in the hotel's stucco exterior revealed adobe brick underneath. Millie brushed her fingers across it. The old hotel should be lovingly placed on a historical register instead of being scheduled for demolition. She huffed at the idea. Regardless of her past connection, what happened to the hotel after she helped Emerson wasn't her concern.

"Emerson Ballard," Millie spoke timidly into the evening air, "did you find your eternal rest?" She would feel better if he had, because what happened to people who went back on promises made to ghosts? As if in answer, a breeze whipped up around her, forming a dust-devil.

"M-i-l-l-i-e," it seemed to whisper

"Ack!" Millie shielded her face and darted back to her car.

People tended to get all freaky over unnatural gusts of wind and rattled papers. Not her, of course. She just didn't want dirt in her hair. Experiencing supernatural phenomena as a child had been a regular occurrence, and Emerson's calming presence had consoled her after her father had left. Millie wasn't calm today, though. She had been either brave or foolish to mingle with a ghost as a child—the jury was still out because her being here, in the same town as Lonny Medina, was already a foolish idea. Being here with a potentially angry ghost was quite possibly insane.

She stared worriedly toward the highway, then glanced at her watch and wondered if he had changed his mind. "Lonny, where are you—are you coming?" When she had called Gila Valley Property Managers LLC and Lonny Medina answered, Millie had fallen off her office chair—it had swiveled right out from under her. Hopefully, they could avoid an awkward business partnership while she oversaw preparations for the hotel's impending sale to GK Investments. Finding an heir was probably key to helping Emerson move on, but if they found one, she would likely lose her job.

A faded blue pickup pulled into the circular drive—the same old truck in which he had driven them to Cluff's Pond as teens. Millie shook her head, tamping down a blush at the memory. Then, wanting to act professional, she inhaled a calming breath and walked to greet Lonny as he stepped from the truck. He had aged well. His straight black hair, long on top but trimmed close at the neckline, was combed but refused to cooperate, as though it rebelled against the guidelines. Very charming. Millie pushed down a grin when he wiped Cheeto-dust from his fingers onto his nicely fitting jeans.

"Millie Crump? I almost didn't recognize you as a blonde."

"It's called highlights. My natural color is still here." She fanned out her hair for his view, and then extended her hand and gave him a firm handshake.

"Really? That's the best you can do for an old friend?" He pulled her in for a hug.

Her heart raced, and for a second it was like old times. Millie pulled away, the intimacy of their contact surprising her. He had no business hugging her like that. She bit back a less-than-professional retort about their "friendship" and instead raised an eyebrow, challenging his comment. "Who are you calling old?"

He laughed, and a wave of heat coursed through her. Staying here and not falling for Lonny again was going to be harder than she'd anticipated. "Do you have keys to get in?" She tapped her toe. At one time, they had loved sneaking inside the cellar. Now she itched to get back home. "You know my firm wants pictures."

"Yeah, sure. But you don't need an excuse. I know your fascination with ghosts and the hotel. I wouldn't dare show up unprepared." Lonny pulled a wad of keys from his pocket and jingled them.

"I'm not sure why," Millie said, "but they insist on detailed pictures of the lobby where Emerson was shot, his private suite, and a few other places." She pulled notes from her bag. "In the kitchen and the root cellar. Why do you think that is?"

"Sounds like they might be looking for the rumored treasure." Lonny moved closer and glanced at her paper.

"That's something I never understood." His nearness sent goosebumps niggling up her arms, and she stepped away. "I mean, what does an old treasure have to do with the hotel today? We never found any hint of treasure, and we were all over this place." Millie rubbed her hands up and down her arms. Maybe she wasn't over Lonny—but his comment about them being friends left her doubting he had ever needed to get over her.

Lonny leaned against the hotel. "I've been doing some research and remember, the Ballard Hotel was famous for weekend cockfights. Even when cockfighting was legal, it drew an unsavory crowd. From what I've learned, Bronco Bill, an outlaw bank robber of the time, frequented the fights here." He swept his hair back. "The treasure was from that, and it could still be here somewhere."

Millie smirked. "It's doubtful that cockfights or an outlaw bank robber had anything to do with Emerson turning into a ghost. And whoever shot him probably took the money themselves."

"You're right, and it doesn't matter whether he was shot by a deputy or by Bronco Bill. It's all rumors and hearsay at this point, but the idea of hidden treasure keeps people's interest, especially since there's no evidence Bronco Bill ever returned for his loot."

"I've done everything I can to find an heir, assuming there is one." Since his call, anyway. Millie touched her hand to his arm, then realized her mistake and pulled away. "I've placed ads in newspapers around the state, letting readers know the place is up for grabs, so-to-speak. In the meantime, I'll work from my hotel room and research the Ballards. But we only have ten days before GK Investments takes over the hotel via the property tax lien."

"And tears it down." Lonny shoved his hands into his pockets. "Forget history; they want to build a fancy restaurant and a butcher shop."

"Yes. Raising gourmet beef is a growing trend," Millie said. "Apparently no one wants a supposed ghost blowing in and scaring people." She lifted a shoulder and smirked, knowing it would rile him.

"Supposed?" Lonny stepped back and assessed her from head to toe. "You've been away for so long you've turned into a city girl." He scrunched his nose as though she stank. "If the place was mine, I'd raise high-end beef without destroying the hotel." He waved toward Mount Graham. "I'd raise cattle on the other side of the barn, closer to BLM land, and sell my gourmet steaks in the hotel restaurant."

"Hotel restaurant? Right. Who would come?" The local ranchers tended to process their own beef.

"This area has grown since you've been away. There are plenty of people who enjoy a good steak and don't mind paying for it. Me included."

She raised an eyebrow but refused to argue her point. "How has your search for an heir gone?"

"Most folks I've asked remember the story of a shootout and the treasure but not much else." He dangled the keys again. "Anyways, you ready to go inside?"

"Absolutely."

He looked at her, his eyebrows lifted. "What?"

"Nothing. Don't mind me." He raised his hands in surrender. "Maybe it's a city thing when your voice sounds all confident, but you appear less than happy about the prospect." He smiled but his eyes mocked her.

How dare he think he knew her. "Me? Scared? Pish." Millie waved the idea away. "You think I'm scared but I'm not." Millie shook her head, not believing the lie herself, but stared him down, daring him to defy her.

"There's nothing to worry about. I've been inside every day this week. Sorry I didn't wait for you, Millie. But I couldn't get it ready and wait at the same time, and this way you know for sure there's nothing to fear."

"I'm not afraid now, nor have I ever been." Not that she would admit to him.

Lonny held up a tarnished skeleton key. "This is the moment you've been waiting for," he teased, then stuck the key in the lock. The click reverberated and the door creaked as he opened it.

Yeah, the moment she had dreaded—facing a possibly angry ghost who demanded restitution for her neglect, and then her humbly offering to help once more. It was the angry ghost part she was most worried about. Millie shuddered and stroked her arms against the sudden chill. Would Emerson let her help or would he just be angry? She rubbed the goosebumps on her arms and started forward.

Pausing on the front step, Millie closed her eyes and inhaled a preparatory breath, trying to get a grip and willing herself to not fall apart in front of Lonny. This was a once-in-a-lifetime opportunity—to see the inside and to say goodbye both to Emerson and to the hotel itself. If GK Investments got their way, and they always did, the hotel would be gone in January. She should be thrilled for this opportunity. Instead, a chill of dread raced through her. Weaker women crumbled under the prospect of facing down an angry ghost. Millie opened her eyes. "Let's do this." She wasn't weak, and she would prove it.

As she stepped inside the cool, dank building, a whoosh of frigid air spiraled around her, blowing her hair across her face and down and around her shoulders, nearly pushing her off her feet. "G-e-t—o-u-t!" the wind rumbled.

Her heart pounded in her chest. "He's going to kill me!" She darted out the door and raced to her Miata.

"Millie, stop!" Lonny called after her.

Two

Lonny jumped into his truck and followed. "What're you running from, Millie?" The Miata sped down the highway toward Phoenix, a full fifteen miles per hour over the speed limit. The Christmas lights in the neighborhoods blurred as he tried to catch up. If she continued like that, she'd end up with a hefty speeding ticket. Lonny pressed cautiously on the gas. "You can't rush off without saying goodbye to my folks." It would crush them.

He knew his parents still held onto hope the two of them would marry, but when he thought of Millie now with her fancy clothes and attitude, he huffed. That was not going to happen. The least he could do, though, was make sure she said a proper goodbye before driving out of their lives again.

Luckily, Millie slowed down inside the Safford city limits and pulled into the parking lot of La Cocina Mexicana. Lonny smiled as she crossed the street and went inside. She never could resist good Mexican food. After parking, he hurried across the street and into the restaurant to talk to the woman he had once dreamed of spending his life with. He spotted her and eased into the seat opposite her. "You raced out of there pretty fast. You afraid of a little wind?"

He grinned, hoping to ease the tension he felt.

"Yeah, well..."

He couldn't believe how she had changed—and not for the better. The old Millie would have grabbed at the chance for an adventure.

She crossed her arms. "To answer your question, yeah, I'm afraid. Who wouldn't be?"

He lifted a shoulder. "You didn't used to be."

She rolled her eyes and heaved a sigh. "I was younger then." She shook her head. "We were younger."

Whatever that had to do with anything. "You should come back to the hotel and check it out. You always dreamed of seeing the inside. It's beautiful."

Millie gazed intently into his eyes and Lonny refused to look away. Her face pinked and she pulled out a menu, staring at it. "It's too dark to take the pictures I need. I'll check into a hotel across the street and meet you tomorrow."

Lonny leaned forward. "I've been inside the Ballard Hotel every day since you called. Nothing's happened. Promise." He sat back and crossed his heart with his finger. "Nothing happened tonight, either, and you know it. So Emerson blew some dust around. So what?"

"So what, nothing. It's been a long day and I'm hungry." Millie used the menu like a shield, hiding her face. "Eating dinner doesn't make me a coward."

"Never said it did."

Their waitress came to the table. She had flashing Christmas bulbs hanging from her ears. "Are you ready to order?"

Lonny leaned over the table and pulled the menu down to uncover Millie's face. "Mind if I stay and eat with you?"

"It's a free country."

"Last I heard."

"I'm just hungry."

"Me, too."

They both ordered, and after the waitress left, Anna Evans, one of Millie's old high school friends approached; her sleek dark hair was pulled back into a loose braid and pinned on her head. Her two kids, KJ and Spencer, were by her side. "Millie Crump, is that you? And Lonny?" Her confusion gave way to assumption. "The two of you back together again. That's wonderful."

Lonny held back a chuckle at the thought of them as a couple now.

Millie's eyebrows dipped. "No. Not *back* together, just *here* together. Anna Sanchez?" A smile rose on Millie's lips. "Where have all the years gone?"

Lonny wondered the same thing.

"It's Anna Evans now." She flashed her ring.

Millie chewed her lip. "Kenny Evans?" She raised her eyebrows.

Anna beamed. "None other."

"I thought he had big plans to leave the Gila Valley and conquer the world."

"He did, and he did." She hugged the children at her side. "After getting his Master's Degree at Cal State, he came back and started his own company. He provides heavy equipment and parts for the mine, farmers, and other businesses who need tractors and the like." She tilted her head. "I keep his books."

"That's impressive," Millie said. "I'm happy for you. Tell Kenny hello from me. Are these your kids?"

"Yes, excuse me." Anna introduced her children and bragged that they'd earned As on their report cards. "We're here for a special treat." She ruffled her older son's hair.

"Super impressive."

That might have been him and Millie if she hadn't disappeared into the Phoenix metropolis fourteen years ago, but seeing her now, he wondered if that was for the best.

"I hear you're in town because of the Ballard Hotel." Anna glanced at Lonny and wrinkled her nose. "Is it true? The place has been wasting away forever. It couldn't be worth much. Why bother?"

Millie answered, "The company I work for, Rumley & Riggs, is overseeing its sale." She gulped as though she felt guilty. "I'm here to prepare the place and take pictures. And to ensure the sale goes through smoothly."

Lonny grabbed his soda and chugged it down to avoid saying something he would regret. Because if she had a conscience, she wouldn't be able to sell the hotel without first helping Emerson.

"Oh, okay," Anna said. "Well, we should totally have lunch while you're in town." She pulled a business card out of her bag and handed it to Millie.

"I'd like that." After Anna left, Millie turned back to Lonny. "It's interesting that the three of you are still here in this tiny town."

Lonny lifted his eyebrows. "As I recall, this was once your tiny town, and one you hadn't wanted to ever leave."

"Yeah." Millie got quiet and stared into the unknown distance.

The waitress brought them their food and they enjoyed a nice meal together. Millie seemed to relax and Lonny was able to successfully put their past behind them for now. After they'd eaten, the waitress brought the bill.

"Let me get that." Lonny pulled out his wallet.

"I'll pay." Millie flashed her credit card and handed it to the waitress. "My company pays for business dinners."

Business. That's all he was. He gulped down the thought. It didn't matter as long as he could get her over to his parents' house. Lonny jumped up and held the chair for her. "After you."

"If I stay, will you be available to go through the hotel records tomorrow? Maybe we'll discover what happened that night and find out if there even is an heir." Millie twisted a strand of her hair.

"I'll clear my schedule." Maybe he should send Anna a thank you basket for getting Millie to stay.

"Will ten tomorrow morning be too early?"

"I'll meet you there." He touched his fingers to his temple in a friendly salute. "I'm glad you've changed your mind about helping Emerson. It really is best since they're tearing down his home, and being inside isn't that bad. Really." He looked at the three nearby motels. "So, which motel is your reservation at?"

"Reservation?" Millie followed him to his truck. "Since when does a person need a reservation in *Safford*?"

She was being ridiculous. He folded his arms across his chest. "Since it's Christmastime and they're having their annual Celebration on Main, and since they're also having a carnival at the fairgrounds with all of the cowboy poets performing."

"If I needed a reservation, don't you think you should have mentioned that fact when you insisted I come?"

"Insist?" He didn't remember insisting. She had jumped at the chance.

"I'm sure there's something available. I'm not sleeping in my car."

"If not," Lonny hesitated, "I have a spare bedroo—"

Millie put a hand up, grimacing. "That's not happening. Why don't I just call a hotel and see if it's even an issue." She pulled out her phone.

Lonny saw her discomfort; regardless of her promise, she wouldn't stay in the Gila Valley long. He needed to get to the real reason he'd asked her to come. "My parents would sure like to see you while you're in town." They had loved each other before, but Millie had changed and he was no longer sure she would agree to see them.

Millie pulled her phone to her face. "I'm sure I won't

be here that long." She turned away, punching in hotel numbers and asking the same questions over and over again, sounding increasingly desperate and annoyed. When she turned back, her face held a stricken appearance as if she actually had seen a ghost.

"Well?" he asked, steeling himself against further hurt. "Where would you prefer staying the night? My place—or the only hotel with available rooms?" Honestly, if she came to his house . . . he didn't know what he thought, but he hadn't expected that look of horror on her face. "Or, I can call my parents and see if you can stay there." It was his parents' constant mention of Millie that had caused him to ask her to come in the first place.

Millie flung her arms into the air. "No, I'm not going to bother your parents this time of night. That's rude to just drop in after all these years and make them put me up."

What was rude was leaving and then not keeping in contact as you'd promised.

"Staying at the Ballard hotel isn't a big deal," she said. "Just because I ran off earlier, you think I'm a big coward, but I'm not. I'll just stay there." Her eyes widened. "Really. It's no big deal. I'll stay there."

She looked as though she'd eaten a bug. It was all Lonny could do to keep from laughing. She had changed so much. In the same instant, he was utterly devastated that she preferred taking her chances in a haunted hotel rather than accepting his hospitality. "Look." He drew closer, working his jaws. "Our ghost is more active two weeks before Christmas. That's now. You might be more comfortable if you stayed somewhere else."

Millie crossed her arms. "Except there is no place else. I'll be fine. Mr. Rumley expects me to get things settled here and be back to Phoenix by Monday. A couple of nights in that old place is nothing." She went to her Miata and then followed as Lonny drove back to the old hotel.

14

The sky was clear, and the glow of a near-full moon lit the hotel like a beacon as he pulled onto the dark, circular drive. It was spooky seeing it like that—like at any moment a dozen ghosts could fly from and around the hotel in a stream of ethereal white. He huffed. That was something Millie would believe. Pure silliness. There was only one ghost that Lonny knew of, and he mostly blew the dust around and knocked things about; although residents had occasionally seen a man through the windows and sworn he glowed. Those were people with overactive imaginations, like Millie.

Lonny parked his truck close to the building and hurried to open Millie's door. Now that he thought about it, he wasn't sure how he felt about her staying the night here by herself. "I haven't been here after dark. There could be coyotes or javelinas or any number of wild animals. Be careful."

"I have a flashlight in my bag." She showed him and put her travel bag over her shoulder and stepped from her car. The brisk air was close to freezing and Millie hugged herself as she hurried to the door.

"Did you leave your coat in your car?" All she had on was a flimsy fake suede thing.

"It appears so."

Her expression wasn't convincing. She probably hadn't thought to bring one. "Take mine for now." Lonny wrapped his warm hoodie over her shoulders.

"Thanks." Millie faced the front door as though facing an adversary. "I can do this," she muttered, not sounding at all confident.

Lonny unlocked the door, walked through the semidarkness to the lobby, and turned on the lights. They flickered and the hazy yellow of antique lightbulbs created eerie, dancing shadows. He looked to see if it bothered Millie.

"Do you think Emerson is angry with me? I mean, staying here would be nothing at all if I was assured he wasn't angry." She stared, wide-eyed, around the lobby. "I mean, I should have tried to find his heir years ago, like I promised, but what more could I have done?"

Lonny clenched his teeth. She could have answered his calls and met with him when he went to Phoenix, for starters. "Like I said, he didn't bother me at all last week. Of course, when the appraiser came ..." Lonny grinned lopsidedly. "Yeah, a couple of gusts and his paperwork was all over the lobby. He took off and refused to come back."

"Of course he did." She raised her eyebrows. "That's pretty sneaky, waiting until after I've come back to tell me that bit of news."

"We had ghost sightings when you lived here. It didn't bother you then, and Emerson's little gust of wind didn't hurt you today, either."

Millie rubbed her arms. "Other than his telling me to get out, the experience was more like an indoor dust devil than a spooky ghost sighting," she conceded.

She said she wasn't scared, but it appeared that her imagination was working overtime. "So, take a look around. I'm sorry there are no Christmas decorations. I know how you love Christmas and all the decorations that go with it. But the place was a mess, and it took more effort to give it a lived-in look than I anticipated." He stood beside her. "We could decorate together if you'd like." That was something they had enjoyed doing as teens.

Uneasy with his nearness, Millie stepped away, resting a hand on her neck and taking in her surroundings. "They're tearing the place down, so there's no need to bother with decorations." Besides, she hadn't celebrated Christmas since moving to Phoenix.

French doors to her immediate left opened into a dining area. From there, a mahogany grand staircase stretched to the second story landing. To its right, the front desk. Beyond that, and underneath the second story landing, the imposing double doors probably led to the Ballard's private suite. To her right was a sitting room with furniture straight from a Jane Austin novel. There was a square table and two chairs in front of the large picture window; a sofa with a brocade print, mahogany legs and back, and a mint green, tufted settee with swirled armrests and mahogany accents.

Millie lowered her hand to her heart. "This is beautiful." She turned for a panoramic view. "A grandfather clock." She had dreamed of owning one and hurried into the sitting room for a closer look.

"I figured you'd like it." Lonny joined her in the parlor. "You're sure you want to stay?"

"Like you said, this has always been a dream of mine. I wouldn't miss this opportunity if my life depended on it." That was a poor choice of words. Millie chewed her nail. "Anyway, I can set up my computer at the front desk."

Lonny shook his head. "There's no point in that."

"What? Why?" Millie walked to the lobby.

"There's no service at all until you get out to the highway."

That explained her dropped call earlier. What would she do in the evenings?

Lonny winced. "You're sure you really want to stay the night here?"

"As sure as I'll ever be." Millie glanced at the light switch across the room. "The electricity works upstairs, too, right?"

"Yeah." He nodded. "Electricity is kind of a package deal; either it works or it doesn't. I've checked the wiring and prepared several rooms in hopes that your buyers will see what an asset the hotel can be. You can have your pick of rooms, but the bathroom is at the end of the hall to your left." He indicated upstairs, took a step toward the door, and then glanced at Millie. "See you tomorrow, yeah? Unless you need something else."

"Nope. I'm fine." Her dream had never included staying at the place overnight. Alone. She ground her teeth together, refusing to beg; she'd done enough of that as a teen. "I'd say you've earned your pay."

Lonny said his goodbyes, and as soon as she saw his headlights disappear, Millie was irritated and feeling abandoned all over again. Ever since she had heard Lonny's voice on the phone, she had fretted that he'd try convincing her to take him back, but he had clearly moved on. He didn't care about her. He never really had.

With her heart palpitating, Millie decided to make sure the place was secure before going upstairs. "Emerson is a friendly ghost," she mumbled, trying to convince herself. "He probably won't show up this late anyway." She wanted to convince herself of that, anyway. "And action is better than sitting and listening to every creak and bump." Old buildings were full of those.

She walked through the French doors to the dining area, turned on the light, and made her way to the kitchen. "See, this is just your ordinary historic hotel. There's nothing spooky." She turned on the kitchen light. No one was there. She looked around appreciatively. "This was pretty fancy for the era." Then she spotted a cute little box and went to it. "Recipes. What a treasure!" They were handwritten in ink and looked like the recipes of the original chef.

Millie put the box away and made her way back through the kitchen and dining area. "This will be charming in the daylight, and I'll laugh at myself for being such a coward." She turned off the lights as she left. "Okay, so I'm talking to myself." She gave a nervous laugh. "Now I need to get upstairs and to my room. And fall asleep." That was the tricky part. She closed the French doors and turned with a start toward a movement at the front desk—a slender gentleman wearing an impeccable blue paisley shirt and a battered old cowboy hat.

Millie's heart leapt into her throat. "Who are you?" She tried to sound authoritative while grabbing her phone from her purse.

"The name's Emerson, darlin'. Welcome to the Ballard Hotel."

The Christmas ghost! But it couldn't be him. Her Christmas ghost was a gust of wind—not a man. Millie dug into her memory, trying to remember if she had seen him in human form, but she couldn't think. Not with him staring at her. "What are you doing here?" The prison was just up the road. She glanced down to find Lonny's number.

"I own this fine establishment." He took a step forward, looking to her left as though someone else was there.

Millie glanced behind her, then put up her palm. "Don't come a step closer. If you don't leave this instant, I'm calling the police." Instead, she hit Lonny's number. "Lonny, it's me. Someone's here. He's tall, around six-foot, dark, straight hair and—" He was quite handsome and well dressed for an inmate—and there wasn't a dial tone. Millie's heart nearly stopped. There was no cell service.

"Now, darlin', don't get yourself all worked up. We have plenty of rooms." He stepped forward.

"Help!" she shouted knowing no one could hear; the adobe walls made sure of that, and they were a mile from the nearest home. Her phone dropped to the floor and she reached in her purse for the only useful thing there. Why hadn't she brought a gun? "I have a weapon and I'm not afraid to use it!" She held her oversized flashlight like a club.

Three

Millie threw her flashlight just as headlights shone through the front window. They distracted her for only a moment, but the stranger had vanished. She held still for a second, the room expanding and the hair prickling at her neckline, and then made a mad dash for the exit. Swinging open the front door, she slammed into something hard. Lonny.

She stepped back and regained her balance. "Someone was here. But he's gone. I threw my flashlight at him. And, and, and—you came back." *I'm so glad.* Millie nestled into Lonny's chest, embarrassed that she was such a wreck.

"Wait." He lifted her chin. "Are you okay?"

"I'm fine." With Lonny's arms wrapped around her, she was surprised at how much better she felt. "Or, I will be. Give me a minute." *Or an hour.*

"Was it our Christmas ghost?" He stroked her hair and her back.

Millie found it delightful and distracting. "Hmm?" Then realizing she was clutching him with a death grip, she stepped away. "Wha-wha-what are you doing here?"

He shrugged, but his mouth twitched. "I got home and then remembered we've always been in this together." He grabbed her hand.

She glanced at his possessive hold. They weren't teens anymore, but Millie was still rattled from the intruder, and Lonny's warm hand felt nice.

"We should make sure it wasn't a trespasser or a prison escapee." He kept hold of her hand and turned on more lights. Together, they searched the hotel. By the back door, dust had come onto the floor, and they saw scuff marks as though someone had gone through.

"Look at that." Millie pointed. "Footprints."

"I've been in and out several times this week. I'm sure these are mine." Lonny checked the door. "It's locked." His movement caused something to move—a scorpion or a mouse.

Millie screamed and pointed at the offending creature. She pressed her other hand to her heart.

Lonny bent down. "You afraid of chicken feathers now?"

"No. I thought it was something else." He didn't need to know what.

"Let's see, did you think it was a scorpion?" Holding the feather by the shaft, he wiggled it in front of her. "Don't let it sting you!" He grinned.

She jumped back. "Cut that out!" How did he remember her fear of scorpions after all these years? That was a detail she wanted to forget.

"Hey, I'm sorry for teasing you, yeah. I know you don't like scorpions." He shrugged. "I had the place exterminated."

"Thank you." His thoughtfulness warmed Millie's heart.

The hotel was secure and they went back to the lobby. Even though it was barely nine, Millie yawned. Stress wore her out.

Lonny winked. "What's next on your agenda, Ms. Crump?"

"I'm staying here," she said weakly. It was crazy but she couldn't leave now. What else would she do, sleep on a park bench?

"Would you like company?" Lonny's eyebrows lifted.

"Yes." Had she answered too soon? Millie searched his expression but saw no judgment. "We could get comforters off the beds and bring them down here. That way we could make sure no one comes in or out without us knowing."

"A sleepover?" Lonny tilted his head, smirking. "Sure."

"Like when we were twelve. Except it won't be in your front yard." And it was super close to her car in case something went wrong.

"As I recall, you got in trouble the next day."

"I refuse to answer that remark." Millie sauntered toward the stairs unwilling to rehash aloud her childhood crush on Lonny and her reasons for being there that night without parental permission. She pulled off her heels. "Come help me get the stuff."

They ran up the stairs, grabbed the bedding off two beds, and hurried back down to the parlor. They moved the settee to make room and set up the sheets and down comforters into rolls like two sleeping bags. The moon shone through sheer curtains on the picture window and added a soft illumination to the room.

The grandfather clock chimed ten as they said their goodnights and closed their eyes.

He was a respectable distance away—it wasn't like she'd bump into Lonny during the night, or accidentally find herself wrapped in his embrace—but what was she doing sleeping only an arm's length away from the man who had broken her heart? And there was the issue of his cologne. It was different from when they were teens, but its scent filled her head with half a dozen thoughts that weren't entirely wholesome. She longed to feel the warmth of his embrace. Her hand, without permission from her, reached out, hoping she would accidentally touch his. All she felt was the oriental rug beneath them.

Millie pursed her lips and turned away. Trying to dredge up feelings from their past was a fool's errand. She needed to get some sleep. Clearly she was tired and not thinking rationally. Tomorrow was Saturday. She would go crazy with no internet and no cell service. She might just go crazy. Period. With all of her irrational temptations, she was driving herself there now.

Even though it was the weekend, she was supposed to send pictures to Mr. Rumley. So to Lonny's steady breathing, she snuggled into her bedroll and made mental lists of things they, or she, could do.

Regardless of her current religious feelings, it only seemed right that the hotel went out in the splendor of holiday lights, if there were any. If not, it was no big deal. They also needed to look through the hotel's files. Millie assumed there were files, but the place had been vacant for as long as she remembered. It was possible the hotel held no personal papers, and they would have to wait until Monday to search county records. That posed a problem. She was expected back to work on Monday. In her haste to come during her days off, she hadn't remembered government offices were closed on weekends.

Millie yawned and fluffed her pillow, rested her head, and tried to sleep. As she started to relax, she became aware of a glow coming from the lobby. The hairs at the nape of her neck bristled. Someone was in there with a flashlight. Her flashlight? She craned her neck around the settee and saw a man standing behind the front desk—the man with the paisley shirt! He was rummaging through something behind the front counter, and he didn't look at all like a ghost.

Slowly, so the intruder wouldn't see her, Millie scooted over and tapped Lonny. "Are you awake?" she whispered.

"Don't say anything." They seriously needed cell service out here.

He turned to look at her. "What?" he mouthed.

She pointed to the lobby.

He nodded. "Reconnaissance One," he whispered, reminding her of when they had played ghost detectives as kids.

With their elbows on the oriental rug, they slipped from their sleeping rolls and edged forward, hidden by the settee. Millie was tempted to jump up and run like the appraiser had done, but she couldn't leave Lonny alone with a possible criminal.

"Let's wait here and see what he's up to," Lonny mouthed.

Millie nodded. Feeling surprisingly awake, she watched the stranger but couldn't quite make out what he was up to from their angle. After what seemed forever, the intruder moved beside the front counter.

"What do you want?" he said, staring toward the front door. "You filthy varmint! You know that's not me." He paused, but then there was a noise at the back door. He vanished with a whirl.

Millie put a hand to her chest, pressing against her anxious heart. That *had* been Emerson. "What is going on?"

"I don't know, but there was definitely a noise."

"Should we go see what it was?"

Lonny's jaw clenched but he didn't say anything.

Millie heard a muffled clank. "Did you hear that? There's someone here." Goosebumps prickled up her arms.

"It's in the cellar, whatever or whoever it is."

Millie shook her head. "But we shouldn't go check it out, right?" She didn't want to meet anyone tonight. Her heart skipped a beat at the idea.

"No." Lonny scooted toward the door. "We need to get

out of here and call the Sheriff."

Millie nodded. Lonny stood and Millie followed his lead, her heartbeat echoing in her ears. Lonny inched his way to the front of the hotel, stopping and listening between steps. They crept through the gloomy parlor. Could a coyote or other animal be stuck in the cellar and unable to find its way out? *There.* She heard it. *A scratching noise.* It was probably an animal. Lonny had mentioned wild animals earlier. As kids they'd accessed the cellar through the wooden hatch outside; the entry was surely more dilapidated now. She was thankful that who or whatever it was couldn't enter the hotel from the cellar.

A bump. That was a bump and not a scratch. Millie clutched Lonny's arm. If it was a human, whoever it was, was fearless going down there in the dark. They'd have to have seen Millie's and Lonny's vehicles parked out front. The wooden floor creaked under Lonny's step. They froze. They were almost to the door. Reaching over, he put a hand over hers. Its warmth was comforting. Sort of. Until she glanced up and saw his worried expression. Every nerve in her body tensed.

They stood still in the darkness, waiting. For what? What were they waiting for? Millie itched to lunge forward and bolt to freedom. But she waited another moment and they started again, finally making it to the door. Lonny opened it and Millie hurried through, turning and watching as he shut and locked it. When she turned back toward her car, the gravel crunched and a light flashed in her eyes.

Millie screamed.

Four

"This is private property," said a male voice, his large silhouette yards from them.

Lonny stepped between Millie and the figure. "Sheriff?" he asked.

"Deputy Sheriff." He stepped forward and out of the shadows. He was easily six-foot tall with broad shoulders and a muscled chest as though he spent an inordinate amount of time at the gym. His nose was wide and flat, and his black hair was cut in a butch style.

Millie's knees wobbled with relief. "You scared me to death!" She clutched her hand to her chest. "You could have made yourself known a little sooner," she scolded.

He raised an eyebrow. "We're trained to not alert criminals that we've found them out, ma'am."

Ignoring his derisive tone, Millie responded, "We're not criminals. I'm Millie Crump, and I'm here as a representative of Rumley & Riggs, property brokers, and this is Lonny Medina, my associate."

"We know each other."

Lonny clenched his jaw—Millie didn't know what his problem was. She extended her hand, thinking the deputy would shake it. Instead, he stood back with his hands to his hips.

"Mousy Millie from high school?" The deputy grinned but it looked more like a sneer in the glow of his flashlight.

Millie huffed. "Yeah. None other." She recognized him now, too, but she wouldn't speak his nickname to his face. "Leonard Begay? You're a deputy now?" Clearly they were hard up if they let him on the force.

"What are you doing here if it's not criminal?" He took a step closer.

Millie stepped back, a shiver coursing through her.

"Now, wait a minute." Lonny put his arm around Millie, drawing her in to keep her warm. She would freeze to death without him around. "We have a legal right to be here."

"Legal or not, I'm not sure it's wise. We've had numerous reports of vandals in the area. They're probably trying to find the treasure before the hotel's torn down. It's not safe."

"Treasure?" Millie made a face. "I'm sure we'll be fine."

"You city folk are all the same. You come to town thinking you're better'n everyone else. Ya think the rules don't apply just because you got a fancy car. But let me tell you, there are any number of dangers out here for a woman by herself. You need to leave."

"She won't be alone," Lonny said. "I'm staying here, too."

"Well, isn't that cozy. And what'll you do if someone breaks in while you're here—wet your pants? Don't put the little lady in harm's way. I'm certain you can think of a better way to show off. One where neither of you end up in a body-bag."

Millie's eyes widened. "A body-bag?" she squeaked.

Lonny had heard rumors about Deputy Begay, but he had never been well-liked, so Lonny had tried giving him the benefit of the doubt. Until now. There was no cause for rudeness or scare tactics. He stepped forward. "Is that a threat, deputy? If so, I'll need to discuss it with Sheriff Adams and see how he feels."

The deputy stepped back but recovered quickly. "No. What I'm sayin', *Mr. Medina*, is that this property has been left vacant and ignored for a long time. It's the kind of property, one with long-vacant buildings, where riffraff like to hang out. And since you and I both know there's no cell service out here, you'd be sitting ducks should you decide to stay."

"That sounds more than logical." Millie backed toward her car, stumbling in the gravel, as though she would leave at Leonard Begay's say so.

She would never have listened to him as a teen. If Millie left town, Lonny knew she wouldn't return, and she hadn't seen his parents yet. He reached out and steadied her as he spoke to the deputy. "With you keeping such a good eye on the property, I feel safer already. We'll stay. Ms. Crump has business to settle before the property is sold."

"Have it your way." Deputy Begay tipped his hat and then stormed into the night.

"What'd you do that for?" Millie hissed, rubbing her arms. "Do you have a death wish or something?" Her teeth chattered in the cold night air, but she scowled and crossed her arms.

"What?" Had she even brought a coat? He put his arm around her and led her back inside of the hotel. "My motive is only for your safety. It's too late to drive to Phoenix tonight; you know that. And you've refused to stay at my house or my parents' house. Besides, I intend to help you keep your promise to Emerson Ballard."

They were just friends, or associates. Whatever that woman wanted to call him, she was completely exasperating, but he couldn't let her just waltz off. Not yet, and not without speaking to his parents. He glanced into her brown eyes but quickly looked away. He couldn't allow himself to get attached again. Mrs. Crump had made Millie's wishes known years ago, and Millie had confirmed them by refusing to answer his calls.

He pulled off his hoodie and wrapped it around her. "I wish I had some coffee to help warm you up. Maybe we should get a few groceries tomorrow; that is, if you plan to see this through." After Millie visited with his parents, they could both go back to their own lives.

"I don't drink coffee anymore," Millie muttered.

"You used to love the stuff." She had changed so much he couldn't pretend he knew her, but there was still that childlike vulnerability in her eyes, and she was still exasperatingly unaware of her needs—who doesn't think to wear a coat in the winter?

"I drink herbal tea now. It's healthier and caffeine gives me migraines."

Herbal tea? That was weird.

"Don't you like herbal tea?"

"Never tried it."

"Well, you should." She gave a half-smile.

It was understandable that they'd developed different tastes after fourteen years, four months, and ten days. Not that he was counting. But no coffee? She used to live on the stuff. They went back to the parlor and crawled inside their bedrolls. Millie kept her roll where she had moved it when Emerson was there. Lonny enjoyed her nearness, maybe too much. He wondered if she felt it, too, because the air between them seemed awkward. Something had changed, but he couldn't begin to guess what.

"Are you okay?" Lonny muttered. "You seem quiet."

"I'm fine. Just tired."

"But there's something on your mind, yeah?"

Millie turned over and glanced at him.

"You can tell me." He put his hand lightly on her shoulder and then forced himself to pull it away.

"Well," she scrunched her face, hesitating, "do you believe in Christmas miracles?"

"I believe in miracles any time of the year," he said. "It's a miracle that we get to reconnect after all this time. Don't you agree? I've thought about you often and wondered if you were okay." He glanced at the twinkling baubles of the chandelier overhead.

"I hadn't thought of that as a miracle, per se. But sure," she said. "I always wondered about you, too. I guess what I mean is, don't you think it'll take a miracle to get Emerson Ballard to quit haunting the hotel? He's been doing it for over a hundred years. And the thing that torments me is wondering what'll happen to him if he doesn't move on and the place gets torn down."

"In that case, I say let's pray for a miracle and then do our best to make it happen. That's all we can do for now."

"I suppose you're right," Millie whispered. "Good night, then."

"Nite." Lonny pulled the comforter over his head and closed his eyes. He couldn't look at Millie only a foot from where he lay. He still felt something for that exasperatingly crazy and stubborn woman, but it was obvious that she had moved on. He would get her over to see his parents tomorrow and then she could do whatever she wanted. He turned his mind to his property management business and all of the appointments he had, then made mental lists of how to accomplish them as he fell asleep.

It was dawn when Lonny rolled over and stared at Millie. Even with the mask of expensive makeup and nails, she was more beautiful than he remembered, but she was definitely a city girl. His heart sank. Even if she did let her defenses down enough that they could start over, as his parents hoped, she would never be content to live here again. And he couldn't leave.

He wanted to brush his fingers over her lips, caress his mouth to hers—and that was a problem. Quietly and quickly he got up and rolled the bedding toward the wall. He needed to get himself into the cold morning air before he did something foolish.

Five

A loud thump awakened Millie. She sat up, struggling against her bedroll while staring through the filtered morning light. "Lonny," she whispered, then looked over to discover his bedroll against the wall. Her heart sank. How could he leave her here? She scampered to the window to make sure his truck was there. It was gone. She was alone. His leaving without waking her was a jerk move. Something creaked and her heart sped up.

She needed to see if someone was there and the best way to do that without finding herself in an unfortunate situation was to go upstairs and look out the windows. First she went to the back door. There were more footprints than yesterday, but they could still be Lonny's prints. Tiptoeing the few feet to the utility closet, she grabbed the broom and swept at the prints. Next time she would know for certain if it was an intruder.

An indistinct thump sounded from the general area of the cellar making the skin around her hairline prickle. Millie was grateful the cellar didn't have an entry into the hotel. She closed her eyes briefly, envisioning the location of the cellar in regards to the main hotel, and then walked carefully to the grand stairway. She heard another creak. Her heart pounded, and she tore upstairs as though being chased by a rabid javelina, slamming the bathroom door shut and locking it. She braced herself against the door for a moment, surveying the room.

"Calm down," she muttered, her breathing shallow. "Nothing's going to happen." The noises could be from the wind blowing something against the old hotel, or even an animal. She went to the window to see; it overlooked the back of the hotel. The old gazebo was still standing. A vague impression came to the surface of her memory—she was sitting in the gazebo crying and a man came to comfort her. It had been Emerson Ballard.

He had talked to her back then, so when he appeared again, she should be able to ask him questions. He should be able to tell her what he needed in order to pass on.

Almost directly below her was the entry to the cellar. The wooden hatch, even more weatherworn than the barn, was lying open. It was highly likely that she was being spooked by groundhogs or any number of wild critters— except a black Jaguar sedan with a classic chrome hood ornament was parked nearby. Gerald Kappel from GK Investments owned such a vehicle.

Her car was out front. Did he know she was there alone or did he assume she merely left her car there? Millie pressed closer to the window pane, trying to get a better look. A dusty Gerald Kappel stepped out of the cellar, carrying a box full of something.

At the sight of him, she raced through the bathroom and chased down the stairs. He had no right to be there, let alone to take things from the property. Nothing was legally his yet. She hurried around the grand stairway and through the hallway to the back door and flung it open. The driver of the Jaguar backed up, nearly hitting the gazebo, and then pulled forward. It was Gerald Kappel.

She waved her hands. "Stop! Stop!"

He sped toward the highway, leaving a trail of billowing dust. Without thinking, she left the hotel and chased after him barefooted, but stepped on a bullhead weed and yelped in pain.

"Okay, okay. I need shoes." Rather than go inside and get her shoes and then come back outside, she removed the sticker and limped to the cellar, being careful of where she stepped. Although the rectangular hole was old and original—the steps going down were made of new wood.

Curious as to what she would find, Millie went in. The smell of the cool dirt filled her with memories, while the dirt floor felt wonderful against her bare feet. She waited for a moment while her eyes adjusted to the darkness. The place was in disarray, with most of the shelving pushed against the earthen side walls and several holes dug near the corners.

On the rustic shelves were a few old pots, what looked like an antique pressure canner, a ladle, and a dozen canning jars. She picked some up and examined them. A few were filled with what looked like whole tomatoes. Others had something green inside.

Millie shuddered and returned the jars to the shelf, then went back up the stairs. She shut the cellar hatch and walked carefully back to the hotel. Other than the antique pressure canner, nothing looked as though it had any value. She went back inside to the hotel parlor, where she'd left her designer heels. The sight of Lonny's bedroll filled her with disappointment. He had agreed to help her today and yet he'd left without waking her or even leaving a note. She was just lucky the intruder was Kappel and not a prison escapee.

His absence was evidence that Mama was right: Men's feelings were as fleeting as a tumbleweed in a windstorm. It didn't matter. He had accomplished all that her company would reimburse him for and had done an excellent job. He didn't owe her more than that and she shouldn't expect more. Except he had promised to help her. But then fourteen years ago he had also promised to come for her, to bring her back, and to marry her. She rolled her eyes, finally glad that he hadn't.

She would do the things on her list by herself. But before tackling that, Millie drove to the highway and set up a lunch appointment with Anna, then returned to the hotel to freshen up. Taking her bag upstairs, she realized a shower was clearly out of the question; ghosts could go through locked doors and Kappel could turn up again. She turned the water on at the sink. It spit and spewed and chugged up the pipe until it flowed timidly into the porcelain basin. Millie splashed cold water onto her face, and then realizing there was no towel, she pulled the hem of her blouse up and dabbed her face dry.

After changing her clothes and reapplying her makeup, and feeling much braver with the Jaguar gone, Millie went to the grand stairway. She had dreamed of being able to walk down this stairway as a girl. She started slowly down, remembering the girlish desires of her heart with every step, until her mother's words came back to her: "Don't fit in with small-town people. They're not going anywhere, and you deserve a better life than I had."

Of course she had meant Lonny, and Millie had stormed off for the day in protest. It didn't matter now, though; her mother had passed away overworked and tired, but she had been right. Lonny was still in Solomon; he hadn't gone anywhere with his life. Sure, he owned his own business, but who cared? It was small, with hardly any overhead, and was merely an extension of what he had done as a teen.

Millie finished descending the stairs with her hand on the mahogany rail, as she might have done a hundred years ago. Standing in the lobby where she'd recently seen Emerson, she called to him. "Emerson, it's Millie Crump. Will you show yourself so we can talk?" She waited a moment for him to respond but didn't see or hear any evidence of him. However, the eeriness inside the hotel was palpable, and Millie had things to accomplish before her lunch date. She hurried out the front door.

The hardware store in Safford was the most pressing item on Millie's list. She bought a chain and lock, and returned to the hotel. Lonny was still absent. She tsked her disappointment in him, drove to the back where the wealthy investor had parked, and then secured the cellar hatch. There would be no more taking things from the hotel until the sale was final.

With her phone in hand, she decided to explore the property and take exterior pictures for her boss before meeting Anna. The barn was at least a quarter mile from the hotel, but perhaps Mr. Rumley would like pictures of it as well. About halfway there, she got an eerie impression and paused, the hair rising on her arms and neck.

The weathered building showed its years, with dry wooden planks that lacked paint and didn't come together well enough to keep the wind out. It was a 3-D picture that belonged in a quaint oil painting, not a spooky dwelling for ghouls. Why then, did the hairs on her neck prickle?

Had someone been out there recently? Millie walked closer, snapping a few pictures. What appeared to be tire tracks circled the building. She couldn't tell for sure, but even if they were, the ground was so hard the tracks could be years or decades old. Maybe when Lonny came back on Monday, they'd go out there together. Monday? What was she thinking? Her boss would never go for that. But somehow she needed to convince him, because now that Millie was here, she needed to keep her promise to Emerson.

For now, the barn creeped her out. She turned around

and hurried toward the hotel. As she did, a sheriff's vehicle pulled onto the property and charged toward her. Millie stopped and watched it approach with alarm. The vehicle turned and pulled to an abrupt stop, the passenger door only three-feet away, the dust billowing behind it. Her heart sank. It was Deputy Begay behind the wheel. She worked her expression into what she hoped was a pleasant smile as he got out and walked around to her.

She nodded a greeting. "Deputy Begay. What brings you out here this morning?"

"I came to check on you." He glanced toward the barn. "Have you been out there—you haven't, right?"

"No. I changed my mind."

He closed his eyes a moment and heaved a breath, seeming relieved. "Good. Sometimes vagrants spend the nights in there. We've even caught a couple of escaped convicts hiding out in the barn."

"I took a few pictures of the outside, but it's kind of creepy." Not that her being there was any of his business, but if she reassured him he might stay away.

"Lonny's not here? Well, I'm glad to see that you're okay—you are okay, right?"

"I'm great. Thank you for your concern." Millie rubbed her arms against a cool breeze.

The deputy stepped forward. "I've been worried about how I scared you last night. I apologize for that." He smiled warmly. "Can I make it up to you by escorting you to the fair today?" He placed his hands behind his back.

She shuddered inwardly at the thought. "That sounds like fun, but I've already made a lunch appointment with Anna Evans."

"Maybe another time then? How long are you staying in town?"

"Just another day or two."

They made pleasantries and then he left after giving

her his business card. "If you change your mind, or if you need anything." He winked. "Give me a call."

"Okay. I will. Thanks." Maybe Leonard had changed. Regardless, Millie had no idea why he would be friendly with her; he hadn't been growing up. She went to her Miata. Two minutes later, she was on her way to an early lunch date with her old friend. Well, old was a less popular term at their age, but childhood friend worked.

This was a short visit of only two days, which really needed to be expanded to the ten days when the sale was official. Unfortunately, Mr. Rumley was right. Other than taking pictures, everything else could be done online. Visiting the county records department on Monday was on her agenda, not her company's—and Millie needed to think of a way to get Mr. Rumley to understand. After Emerson moved on, she could go home and forget she ever lived here. She sighed. Except the people were nice and she didn't want to forget them. Not really.

By eleven-thirty, Anna and Millie were at a café on Main Street in Safford. The place was new to Millie. Main Street had changed and seemed to thrive. Anna pulled her phone out of her bag and put it on vibrate. "I always like to silence my phone for lunch, it gives me a short break from all the chaos at home." She smiled and put her phone back in her bag. Taking Anna's lead, Millie put her phone on vibrate as well.

"I always thought there was something going on with you and that hotel," Anna said as they ate. "You and Lonny were always hanging around over there. It was so spooky. If someone wants the place, why don't you just let them have it?"

"I will." Millie nodded. "But back in high school, I made a promise. I've got to at least try to keep that promise before the prospective owners tear the place down."

"Good riddance." Anna dipped a French fry in catsup

and ate it. "The place is an eyesore. My Kenny can clean up that property real good." Anna raised her eyebrows in anticipation of getting new business.

"After the sale becomes final." Millie wouldn't be talked out of helping Emerson, and then she remembered her visitor. "Hey, what's with Lenard the Letch? He's a deputy sheriff?" She didn't have any doubt Anna would share information if she had it.

"Yeah." Anna waved the issue away. "He's not that guy anymore." She bit into her burger and then smiled slyly. "He's matured quite nicely if you ask me. But seriously, being with the sheriff's department has really straightened him out."

"Impressive." Millie nodded thoughtfully. He must have just been on his guard the other night or showing off. Millie relaxed. Anna was a good judge of character. Maybe she should take him up on his offer of taking her to the fair.

"I hear he's always having problems with intruders out at the old hotel property. All the locals know to stay away. Too dangerous." Anna leaned over the table. "Even though it was creepy, Kenny and I went out to the barn once." She wiggled her eyebrows. "It was a great make-out spot. But it smelled off. Like death. We never went again."

Millie filed the death smell away for further consideration. "You do know the hotel is haunted, right?" How had Kenny talked Anna into going out there?

Anna waved a hand and rolled her eyes. "Believe me when I tell you the living are more dangerous than a silly ghost."

Millie briefly wondered what her friend meant, but said, "I spent the night there last night and I didn't see anyone— except Deputy Begay." It had still been authentically spooky.

"Alone?" Anna's eyebrows dipped with concern.

Oops, that was the wrong thing to say. Millie shook her head. "It doesn't matter—It was no big deal—Lonny would have done the same for you if you'd seen a ghost." Except he'd left her there with an intruder. That had been truly frightening.

Anna's eyes opened wide. "You really saw the ghost?"

Okay, so this conversation was digressing and wasn't getting her the information she needed. Millie changed the subject. "The town has grown so much since I left. I hardly know where to go for information about Emerson Ballard."

"Maybe ask your ghost." Anna smiled wryly. "Are you sure it wasn't a homeless person or even an escaped convict? Or maybe the "ghost of Emerson Ballard" is just a code name for Lonny. Am I right?" Anna laughed.

"Oh, stop that!" Millie's face and neck heated; but the truth was, Lonny had left early and hadn't bothered to call.

Anna ate another fry, brightening with an idea. "Really, in all seriousness, you're in luck. The cowboy poets and storytellers are in town for Christmas on Main Street. They know more about that era than anyone. You should ask them."

"Okay, yeah, that's a good idea." This was why Millie had come to the Gila Valley—to find credible sources—not to stay in haunted hotels or to hang out with Lonny.

"They're out at the fair grounds today. There's a carnival and a country craft fair."

"So I should just go out to the fairgrounds and introduce myself? Won't that be weird? It's not like I know them."

"They won't bite." Anna took a drink of her soda.

"You wanna come?"

"Oh, heavens no." Anna waved a hand. "I'm on Mom-duty as soon as I get back. Plus, I've got payroll."

After lunch, Millie stayed at the cafe and looked up the cowboy poets on the internet. Their program started at three. With Anna's changed opinion of Deputy Begay on her mind, she called him and agreed to meet him there at two-thirty.

Six

"Thanks for meeting me here," Millie said. "The fair is more fun when you share it with someone." Her heart panged with regret. Regret that Lonny hadn't asked her.

"The pleasure is all mine." Leonard tipped his hat. "Did you and Lonny have an argument?—it's none of my business and I'm grateful for any reason that led you to call." He looked down at her with kindness.

"No. It's nothing like that. My company hired his to prepare the property for sale. He had other commitments today." She thought he did, anyway. He'd been gone longer than she had anticipated for a Saturday.

They walked toward the stage area, visiting and getting reacquainted with one another. "I'd be honored if you'd skip all the formalities and call me Len. It's what my friends call me."

"Then Len it is." Millie had judged him wrongly. Len was nice and polite. Anna was right, he was strikingly handsome with his boot-cut jeans and nicely sculpted sweater-shirt. His military haircut only added to his looks.

"Do you mind if I hold your hand so we don't get separated in the crowd?"

"Oh, okay." Millie didn't want to hold his hand, but remembering with shame the rumors that had spread about him in high school, and his current endorsement from Anna, she agreed.

Pictures of Buckshot Bill, Donny Derringer, and Cowgirl Kate were on posters around the fairgrounds. Millie inhaled deeply. "I love the smells of Indian fry bread and roasted chili peppers. Everything is mingled with the sweet scent of cotton candy—it brings such good memories."

The sounds of people screaming on the rides almost drowned out the loud carnival music, but that was the charm of the fair. Len and Millie walked through the 4-H area with the livestock, drawing her thoughts to Lonny, and then how he'd left her alone this morning.

"The stage is this way." Len placed his hand lightly against her back as he led them toward the nearly full bleachers. His touching her seemed too personal for friend status, but she'd had blind dates who also liked physical contact. Millie felt bad for her behavior toward him growing up and vowed to treat him nicer and to give him the benefit of her doubts.

"Let's sit somewhere out of the way." She didn't really care about the performance.

"Oh, yeah. I've seen this group every year when they come to town. You'll really enjoy 'em." Len held her hand again and led the way to a center bleacher halfway up.

The show started with the bang of cap guns and ballads of the Old West. They did seem to know a lot about the era and the area. Len seemed mesmerized and Millie sat forward, listening. When Cowgirl Kate recited a ballad about Bronco Bill, her arms tingled with excitement. She might actually leave here with concrete information about Emerson Ballard.

After their show, Len led the way, pushing toward where the poets were selling and signing copies of their

CDs. "You've got to buy this one." He showed it to Millie. "It's my favorite." He picked up a different one. "This one is new. I'll take it." He pulled out his wallet and paid Buckshot Bill for the CD. "My friend here would like to talk to you."

Millie stepped closer. "Hi! Your performances were great." Starting with a compliment never hurt. "The three of you seem to know a lot about the area."

"Yes," Donny Derringer said. They were all smiles and continued talking and selling CDs to their fans. "You won't find three people who know more about the area than we do."

"May I have some of your time to talk about the Ballard Hotel? After you're through here, of course." Millie handed them cash for the CD Leonard recommended. This wasn't her style, but they'd be more receptive if they thought it was.

"The Ballard Hotel in Solomon?" Cowgirl Kate autographed Millie's CD and handed it back.

"Yes." Millie nodded, feeling hopeful. "That's the one."

"We don't have time today, darlin," Buckshot Bill said. "We're going out for dinner with the other performers before our evening show. Perhaps tomorrow."

"Tomorrow will work." Millie would make herself available. "What time?"

"You look like you're from the city—how about you take us out to lunch while we talk. There's a great Mexican food place in town."

"Noon, then?" Millie couldn't believe these old toots were squeezing a meal out of her.

After making the arrangements, Len led her through the fair. They rode a few of the rides, and Len threw rings over soda bottles and won her a small stuffed bear. His pager buzzed and he looked at it, concern on his face. "Duty calls," he said. "Are you staying the night at the old hotel again? Would you like me to drop you off or escort you inside?" He placed his hand lightly on her shoulder.

"You work nights?"

"Sometimes."

Millie didn't like the idea of being at the hotel alone, especially after seeing Kappel there. "I'm not ready to go back yet, but I appreciate the offer." She gave him a quick hug and pulled away. "I really appreciate getting to know you better." He was a lot nicer than she remembered.

"Maybe we can meet up again before you head back to Phoenix?" He raised his eyebrows.

"I'd like that." Millie watched as Len headed toward his SUV and then turned and went to the building where they judged canned goods and art.

When she came out of the metal building it was starting to get dark. Lonny still hadn't contacted her, and being at the fair had lost its charm. She drove back toward Safford, parked in a hotel parking lot and started calling again for a room. "We have no rooms available," was everyone's response. *There's no room at the inn.* Millie surprised herself with the foreign thought. *Does that mean I should sleep in the Ballard's barn?* Not on her life. She pulled Anna's card from her bag and stared at it, but she couldn't do it. Millie was too proud to call and ask Anna, a friend she hadn't seen or talked to since she was a teen, if she had room for a guest.

She started her car and pulled onto the highway, turning toward Solomon.

All of the Gila Valley towns were small, but driving from one to the other was similar to driving from Phoenix to Scottsdale, time-wise. Only the scenery was different. And the people. Millie liked the anonymity of city life. No one knew anyone else's business, and no one cared to know. It had been tough having the whole school know that her father had run out on her and Mama.

Caught up in her thoughts, Millie ended up in her

old neighborhood. The tiny house where she had lived was aglow with Christmas lights. It made visible the large missing chunks of stucco near the foundation and the peeling paint along the eves. Many of the homes in this neighborhood were in similar disrepair, yet they all shone with signs of the Christmas season. She gulped back her guilt. As a child her faith had filled her, but losing her father, her home, her friends, and Lonny all in the same year had knocked it out of her. There hadn't been anything to celebrate after that.

With the deputy's warnings, staying alone at the old hotel was out of the question. It was too spooky and Anna was right: sometimes the living were scarier than a ghost. She would only go inside to get her bags. Millie drove to the old hotel breathing in Christmas memories of Lonny and the Medinas and feeling more at peace. When she pulled in the drive, though, lights flickered in the barn. The memory of her earlier feelings creeped up her spine, and she circled back onto the highway. She would stay in these clothes for the night.

There was no place for her to go but she drove on, down the highway and through familiar neighborhoods, her car seeming to stop of its own volition only minutes later. In front of her was the tiny whitewashed building with a cross in the bell tower; her second home as a girl. The shadowed building chided her for her neglect, and she wouldn't go in. She couldn't.

"Whatever." Millie left the car running and the heater blasting, reclined the seat, and curled herself into a ball for maximum warmth. Sleep was an impossible dream, but she would shut her eyes and pretend.

Seven

Where was that woman? Had she gone back to Phoenix without so much as a text? Lonny left the hotel and put Millie's travel bag on the floor of his truck, dismissing the idea that she'd left town without her things. It caused him greater concern that no one knew her whereabouts.

Although there were lights in the barn, he was too worried about Millie to concern himself, and it looked as though the sheriff's department had it under control; one of their vehicles was nearby. He drove away from the hotel. When he reached the highway, he drove to the nicer Solomon neighborhoods and slowed as he passed Leonard Begay's place, but her red Miata wasn't there, either.

He grabbed his phone. "Hey, Anna, it's Lonny again. Have you heard any more from Millie? Yes, I went out to the fairgrounds, and the cowboy poets had talked with her." He left out the part that she was with Leonard Begay. "They had no idea where she was going after that. I've called her several times, and texted her, but she isn't responding." He felt like an overprotective loser, but he had an uneasy feeling, and his parents still expected to see Millie. He didn't want to disappoint his father—not again.

"No, it's all right. I'm sure she's safe and everything is okay." Lonny hung up, convinced that something was wrong. Pulling off the side of the road for a moment, he said a quick prayer. He needed to find her. She was too stubborn to ask for help and too likely to freeze to death without a coat.

He said amen and drove through the streets of Solomon with a sense of resolute calm. It was only out of habit that he glanced at the church, and there was her car. He stopped and stared. It was in the church parking lot, of all places—the windows steamy, and the motor running. His heartbeat slammed into his throat; he slammed the truck into park and jumped out.

She was in the car but something was wrong. Was the car somehow filling with carbon monoxide? "Millie!" He banged on the window, panic rising. He called her name again, then tried the door. It was locked. What was she thinking? He pounded on the window again. "Millie, wake up!" She stirred, and he heaved a sigh of relief. She was only sleeping. But why was she sleeping in her car like some homeless person? It would get below freezing before morning. He banged the window again. "Millie, unlock the door!"

She sat up, scrunching her eyes as though she'd been sleeping for a while. "Lonny?" She wiped her hands across her face and rolled down her window, bracing against the whoosh of cold air. "What are you doing here?"

"What am I doing here?" What did she think? "I've been chasing you all over town and trying to catch up to you—didn't you get my note? I texted you five times, and I've called, too. Why didn't you answer your phone?" His heart was racing, but he took a deep breath and forced himself to calm down. She was safe.

"I didn't get any texts and I certainly didn't get a call." Millie pulled her phone from her bag. "See?" She showed it to him, but then saw the list of unanswered calls and texts. "I'm sorry. I don't know what happened—oh, yeah. I put it on silent when I was with Anna." She made a face. "Sorry."

"Don't worry about it. But, hey, I talked to my parents, and you can stay there until Monday. If you still want to stay after that, you'll have your pick of hotels."

"My boss expects me in the office on Monday—and I can't put your parents out." Millie brushed her hands through her hair. "I haven't talked to them since I left. They probably hate me."

"They don't hate you; they ask about you all the time. They're excited to see you again." He lifted his eyebrows. "You could stay at my place if you'd rather, but you're not staying the night in your car. You'd freeze."

She stroked her forehead, wincing. "I don't have my bags or anything. They're still at the Ballard hotel."

He rubbed his hands up and down his arms, trying to warm them. "I got them for you. They're in the truck." He nodded toward his vehicle, hoping she would come before he got hypothermia.

Millie turned off the car motor and stepped from her Miata. The frigid wind whipped around her. "Whoa, that's cold!" Her teeth chattered and she slipped back into her seat. "I'll meet you there. I don't want to leave my car here."

Lonny got into his truck, and she followed him to his parents' house. Once there, Millie hesitated. "Are you sure this is going to be okay?"

Lonny would not let her get this close and then back out. "The guest room is all set up." He grabbed her bag, and with his arm around her shoulders, he led the way. Millie stopped at the door, taking note of his parents' Christmas lights. They were strung around the front window and enshrouded a small manger on the sill inside. She reached out as if to touch them.

"After all these years it's still the same," she whispered

as though this was a sacred place. "This is so kind of them."

His heart softened. "You know they've always loved you like a daughter." He opened the door and motioned for her to enter. "They go to bed early nowadays, but they want you to feel at home." He led the way to the guest room. It was small, with a worn single bed draped in a simple blue bedspread and a small dresser against the wall.

"This is your old room."

He nodded. "Yeah." He put her suitcase on the dresser. "You can put your things inside or use the closet. Whatever you'd like." There was so much he wanted to say to her—to tell her about the last fourteen years—each small victory and his myriad setbacks. "So, I own the place a few doors down now." He swept his hair back, not knowing what else to do. "If you need anything . . ." He didn't even know how to finish. This was what he'd always dreamed of, and he didn't even know how to talk to her anymore. They were standing too close. He wanted to touch her, to hold her, but that was not going to happen. They were *associates*. He put his hands in his pockets.

She gazed at him questioningly, her head slightly turned. "I'll be fine, I'm sure." She moved away from him and sat on the edge of the bed. "Will you be here tomorrow?"

That was kind of an odd question. He wouldn't dump her here and then make his parents play host and hostess by themselves. "Yeah. Breakfast is at eight and then Church at ten. They're excited for you to come with us."

"What?" Millie glared, as though she'd never been inside of a church.

"If you don't want to, I can tell them. I mean, they wouldn't want to force you." Sheesh. He hadn't expected that reaction.

She gave him a forced smile. "I'll go," she said and looked down. "It's not like I haven't been inside a church since I moved away."

No, it just seemed that way. She was acting too guilty.

This was really getting awkward. Why didn't he leave already? "Well, okay then. I hope you sleep well. I'll see you in the morning." He turned and left the room, closing the door behind him.

Eight

The aroma of frying eggs and chorizo filled the room, and the sound of roosters greeted the new day. Millie inhaled deeply, the scent and sounds taking her back to her childhood and Mrs. Medina's famous Chilaquiles and Huevos Rancheros with chorizo, frijoles and rice. She got up and dressed, then stood at the dresser and reapplied her makeup to make sure she looked her absolute best, and walked timidly out to greet the Medinas.

Mr. Medina looked thinner than she remembered; he always loved sitting on the sofa and watching the news on TV. Mrs. Medina was in the kitchen, her graying hair tied in a bun on her head. She still appeared soft and huggable, and she still wore a red-checkered apron. They both seemed to see her at the same time. Mrs. Medina rushed to greet her, and Mr. Medina stood. *"Hija!"* Mrs. Medina gave her a huge embrace.

"Mami." Millie blinked back tears, her invisible walls crumbling, as she hugged the old woman in greeting.

Mr. Medina shuffled forward, his eyes brimming. *"Hija,* you are home at last."

"Papi." Millie embraced the frail man. "Oh, *Papi,* I have

missed you!" They embraced for a moment longer, then Mr. Medina took her hand in his and walked to the blue sofa. It took him a moment to settle into it.

"Now come and tell me why all these years you have not come to visit?" He patted the sofa. His voice was stern, but Millie felt the pain in his words. They had missed her as much as she had missed them.

She sat beside him, his little *"Hija,"* and wished to take his hurt away. "I'm so sorry!" All the love for this couple rushed back to her and her voice quavered. "Mama would not let me come." She wiped her arm across her eyes. "She said it would be too painful, that I needed to move on."

He patted her hand. "That is not right, *Hija*. When you are a little chicken alone in a desert, you need all your loved ones near. We should have been there for you and we wanted to be." He paused, seeming to consider his words. "Is that also why you didn't marry our Lonny?"

"*Marido!* Husband!" Mrs. Medina scolded. "That is not our business." She wiped her hands on her apron, her expression turning remorseful.

"*Querida,* Dear, you are right, as always." He gave her a smile, patted Millie's hand again and released it. "We are glad you are back and are honored to have you in our home."

Mrs. Medina wiped her hands on her apron. "Lonny is in the pasture feeding the stock if you would let him know breakfast is ready."

"*Sí, Mami.*" Had Lonny been here this whole time? She walked outside. There were six head of cattle in the five-acre pasture, and they nudged around Lonny, anxious to eat. He held several flakes of hay and peeled them apart, spreading them along the feeding trough. The morning air was cool and the breeze made it nippy, and as she walked to him, Millie rubbed her arms at the chilly realization that she should have purchased a coat yesterday. "Are these your cattle or do you take care of them for your folks?"

"You forgot to bring your coat." Lonny took off his jacket and put it over Millie's shoulders. "They let me keep them here, rent free, as long as I share fresh beef when I have it." He smiled as though it was a joke.

Lonny's warm jacket smelled like a thousand memories and made her head swim in confusion. She was only here for a few days, not a lifetime. *Do not let yourself get caught in his orbit again.* "Um," she said, "breakfast is ready. Your mom sent me out to tell you." She couldn't help but bring her arm up and inhale the scent of his jacket sleeve, then she turned around and went inside with Lonny following beside her.

After they said grace and began eating, Millie wondered if Lonny had thought to ask his parents for information on their ghost. "Do you know anything about the Ballard hotel?" she asked them. "I know it was before your time, of course it was, but maybe people had been more interested in its history before."

"Someone came and tried to open the hotel for business once." Mr. Medina tore a piece of his tortilla. "That's why it has newer plumbing."

"He only lasted until a couple weeks before Christmas." Mrs. Medina shook her head at the memory. "He spent all that money on the place, had the grand opening signs up and everything. The newspaper even interviewed him. One day he was gone, and no one ever knew what happened."

"That is so strange." It fit in with Emerson's timeline of showing up at Christmastime, though.

Neither of them had much more to say about the hotel or Emerson Ballard, but Millie thanked them anyway. She made sure to savor and appreciate the wonderful food Mrs. Medina had surely gone to extra effort to make especially for her.

"Look at the time," Mrs. Medina said. "It is time to go."

She looked at Millie with wide-eyed hopefulness. "Will you attend services with us?"

"I would be honored," she said. How could she not go with the two most lovely people in the world? Her current views on religion and God had no bearing on the situation.

"You should drive there with our son." Mr. Medina winked. "We will be along as soon as we're able."

"Do you need help, *Papi*?" Lonny stepped toward him.

"We are not completely unable to care for ourselves," he responded. "You two, go." He swished them away with his hands and a twinkle in his eyes.

"All right, all right." Lonny hesitantly put his hand on Millie's shoulder and sent her an apologetic glance.

Whatever his reasons for not coming for her after he graduated didn't seem as important, and Millie relished his nearness as they walked outside. He opened the truck door for her and then got in.

"Sorry about that," he said. "They have this idea that we're still teenagers." He gave her a half smile.

"Don't worry about it," Millie said, wishing she could take her own advice. She chewed at a nail, then realizing the error, she stuffed her hands underneath her.

Father Garcia greeted Millie like a lost soul returned. That, and the aroma of burning candles, brought out feelings she didn't know how to categorize. It made her uncomfortable. The Medinas soon joined them on the pew and they celebrated the birth of Christ together.

The divorce of Millie's parents' and the subsequent move to Phoenix had made her angry with her mom and with God; it had separated her from Lonny and his parents, and kept her from figuring out what her ghost needed in order to move on. But foremost in her heart at that moment was the warm feeling of being surrounded by love. She felt the light of pure joy at knowing the Medinas had never stopped loving her. And Lonny? She tentatively moved her hand and rested it on top of his, glancing up at him. He smiled and took her hand in his, bringing it to his lips for a soft kiss.

As the service was nearing it's end, and remembering her lunch commitment, she leaned over and whispered to him, "After this is over, I'm meeting the cowboy poets for lunch. You wanna come?"

"I can't." He made an apologetic face but gave no other explanation.

Millie nodded and tried not to show her disappointment. It was perfectly okay. He couldn't change his whole life just because she had barged into town.

After returning to the Medinas' from worship services, Millie excused herself and drove toward Safford. She stared out the windshield, seeing only the road before her. Despite the love she felt from the Medinas, it had been difficult going to church and feeling as though God's judgments were on her. It was irrational, but it felt like everyone knew it was her first time in a church since leaving Solomon. As she pulled into the parking lot and started toward the restaurant, a county sheriff vehicle swung into the lot and parked nearby.

Millie groaned.

Nine

Deputy Begay got out, hurrying toward her.

Millie didn't understand why he would take it upon himself to just show up, and she bristled at the awkwardness of seeing him unexpectedly.

"I'm glad I got here in time. There was an incident out on the 89." He took his hat off and swept his hand through his hair. "You don't want to hear about it. I'm just glad I made it in time to walk you inside." He peered down at her, smiling like a Cheshire cat.

Millie hadn't invited him and wondered if he had read more into their few hours at the fair than she had. But she wouldn't be hateful to him, so she took a breath and smiled. "You couldn't have timed it better." She stiffened when he put his hand on her shoulder, but she forced herself to relax as they walked in together.

Deputy Begay let the waitress know there would be three extras. The waitress led them to a large table, then brought them complimentary chips and salsa. She took out her pad and took their drink order.

"You were always too busy with Lonny in high school. I never stood a chance at getting a date with you. I'm sure glad to have the opportunity now."

"Oh?" Her nerves twitched as if she were in a weird dream. How had she misled the deputy into thinking he was invited or that this was a date? But it didn't matter at this point. She needed to treat him nicely.

"What did you end up doing with the stuffed animal I won for you?"

Millie blinked, her mind racing for a good answer. "I have a special place in mind for it at home." It was currently in the trunk of her car.

"I wish you didn't have to go back to Phoenix." He touched her arm. "We need more good people here, like you."

"I should be back in Phoenix now," Millie said.

"What exactly is your business with the hotel?"

"You know the place is haunted, right?" She watched his expression.

"I do know the rumors. I've never come across any spirits myself, and there's so much riffraff out there nowadays that I have plenty of occasion to be out there. That's why I was concerned for you the other night."

"Have you been inside the hotel, then?"

"I don't have any reason to go inside. My job is to keep vandals off the property. It'll be a relief to have someone else overseeing the place. The new owners going to fix it up?"

"They're tearing it down." Millie then told the story of the prospective owners' mission. Without mentioning her association with Emerson, she told of her age-old, but now conflicting, promise to find an heir to the property. Like Anna, he assumed the promise was made to Lonny.

"At this point we don't even know if Emerson Ballard was married or if he had children. If not, another close relative might be interested. The cowboy poets may know something about Emerson, and if they do, I'll be on my way back home tonight." And maybe jobless by Christmas.

"Let's hope they don't know, then." Deputy Begay winked and took a swig of his drink.

Millie smiled.

The cowboy poets came bursting through the door in full costume, behaving as though this was one of their venues. "Yee-haw! Let's get this party started!" Chuckling, Millie stood and waved them over.

"I'm Millie Crump and this is Deputy Leonard Begay." Millie shook their hands. "Remind me again of your stage names."

"I'm Donny Derringer." He took off his cowboy hat and swooped in a grand bow.

"I'm Cowgirl Kate." She took her toy gun and lifted it into the air. "Pow! Pow! Pow!" She made the motions of firing the toy repeatedly. "I'm the fastest gun in these here parts. This here's been my best friend for fifty-plus years." She indicated the man to her left. "Please welcome Buckshot Bill!" The people in the restaurant applauded. The trio took a bow and then sat at the table with Millie.

Deputy Begay nudged Millie. "I thought you were going to call me Len."

"That's right. Len," Millie repeated. "Len Begay." She smiled at the aging entertainers. "He's off duty."

"This is the fine gentleman who escorted you to our show yesterday." Cowgirl Kate shook his hand.

"I'm one of your biggest fans." He pulled several CDs from his pocket. "Will you autograph these?"

Lunch with Buckshot Bill, Donny Derringer, and Cowgirl Kate was entertaining, to say the least. They were famous enough in the area that fans kept wanting their autographs. Some asked them to write poems about particular ancestors who had helped settle the area.

The historians were primarily entertainers, and that's how they got their pay. It wasn't surprising that they used the lunch as a promotional opportunity, but when lunch was nearly over and Millie hadn't gotten any answers, she was feeling used. She didn't like it.

"So, do you know anything about Emerson Ballard? Was he married? It seems unlikely that a single man would buy and run a hotel back then." Millie wiped her mouth on her napkin and placed it over her plate.

"Married?" Cowgirl Kate pulled a pad of paper and pen from her bag. "That'd make a great ballad."

Millie suppressed her annoyance. "Do you know anything helpful about the Ballard Hotel?"

"We don't have any specific knowledge other than Buffalo Bill went there," Buckshot Bill said. "Solomonville is what the town was called back then, and it was barely settled. Arizona was still a territory."

Cowgirl Kate looked up from her writing. "There's a couple who still lives here—good friends of ours. They probably know more about the Ballard Hotel than we do. Clive Palmer's his name. Wife's name is Lillian. You should give 'em a call. Tell 'em that we sent you."

"Sounds like a great idea, thanks." Millie waved for the waitress to bring the bill, and then got the Palmers' contact information. The poets offered Millie free tickets to their afternoon show to compensate for the lunch. "I'd love to," she said, "but I've got to focus on my research." No way was she sitting through another performance.

"Are you sure?" Deputy Begay quizzed. "How could we miss an opportunity like this?"

"I really can't. My time is limited." She wondered if this was the reason he had come, to spend personal time with the poets. Regardless of his disappointment, she held firm.

Cowgirl Kate tipped her pink hat. "Darlin', I hope the Palmers have the information you're after."

"Happy trails to you." The two men bowed deeply,

their hats to their chest, and then the three of them left.

Before speaking to Deputy Begay or leaving, Millie pulled out her phone and punched in the Palmers' number. Luckily, they were in and agreed to speak with her. "Okay, well, I've gotta go," she told him. "They've agreed to meet me in a half hour. It'll probably take that long to get to Central."

"Every bit," he agreed. "But I'd love to come with you." He walked with her toward the door.

"Honestly, you don't need to come along." He really had nothing to do with her search, so she didn't understand why he'd come to begin with. Maybe his motivation was to have lunch with the poets and to get their autographs. "I've got this. You probably have work . . . or, someone to get back to," Millie said, realizing she didn't know much about the deputy. They had spent most of their time discussing her and the hotel.

"I'm off duty." He climbed into the passenger side of her Miata without the slightest encouragement.

Millie started the car and sped toward Central.

"You do remember that we're sticklers for the speed limit around here," Deputy Begay said. "I'd hate to have to give you a speeding ticket."

"Sorry." Millie despised acting as though she was meek and submissive, but she did remember that little fact, and slowed to the speed limit.

They arrived safely at the Palmers' faded turquoise home, and the frail couple let them in. The furnishings were a 1930s style but in good condition. The place had the acrid scent of mothballs. After a meandering conversation involving way too much reminiscing for Millie's comfort, they had a little more information.

Mr. Palmer placed his hands on his knees. "We used to learn about Solomon's history in school, and as I recall, Emerson Ballard did have a wife. She ran the hotel while

Emerson, that's his first name, he farmed and worked for the mine. I don't think he was a miner though. I think he was a foreman or maybe he shipped supplies to the mine. Something." Mr. Palmer glanced over at his wife, who had fallen asleep beside him. "Well, I got to get this pretty little lady in for her nap. Was there anything more you needed?" He softly patted his wife's hand, awakening her. "Come on, sweetheart. Let's get you comfortable."

Millie stood, preparing to leave. "One more thing," she asked. "Do you remember Mrs. Ballard's name?"

Mr. Palmer put a fist over his mouth, thinking. "I don't rightly know," he said. With an arm around his wife's shoulders, he helped her to stand. "I'll let you see yourselves out." With that, he and his wife disappeared around the corner.

Millie wanted to grit her teeth. She had spent the whole afternoon in search of information, and only knew that Emerson Ballard may have been married.

She started the car. "I'm going to be in so much trouble if my boss finds out I'm trying to find an heir to the hotel. It'll lose him the business."

"Not that I'm encouraging you to go out there, but why don't you just ask the ghost of Emerson what he needs in order to move on?"

"It's not as simple as that. I attempted calling for him yesterday and he didn't show." Millie tried remembering how often she had seen Emerson in human form, but a lot of that time of her life was a foggy mess that she had put behind her in order to heal. "I'll see if I can get his attention when I get out there again. He usually gusts in and out."

Len turned toward her. "So, how does your boss not know you're looking for an heir? I thought he paid for the newspaper ads."

"Well, sure he did, but that's a legality. He still expects me to be at work tomorrow. In Phoenix. All he wanted was the place straightened and a few pictures taken for our books."

"I could have sent you pictures." Deputy Begay shrugged. "Anyone could have sent you pictures. What's your true reason for being here?"

"My true reason?" Millie was suddenly irritated at the predicament she had put herself into.

No one other than Lonny seemed to take her seriously in her search to help Emerson. She should have stayed home, but the moment she had heard Lonny's voice, she was up and packing. She wouldn't admit that to Len, though.

"You're absolutely right. Whether there's an heir or not has nothing to do with my company's business, and I haven't found a reason compelling enough that my boss will let me stay. I'll probably leave early in the morning. Be to work by eight." The thought made her sick with worry. She pulled into the restaurant parking lot and stopped next to Deputy Begay's vehicle.

Len smirked. "That's hardly practical. You'd have to leave in the morning by five." He took her hand then, seeming contrite. "I prefer you move here and we can get to know one another better. If you must leave, you should leave tonight before the sun goes down. I'd hate to think of you driving those windy roads after dark."

"I have no intentions of moving here, and I can take care of myself. Thank you, though." Millie dipped her eyebrows wondering what was going on in his brain.

Ten

Mr. Medina clicked off the TV with the remote. "Call your boss tonight and leave a message. Tell him your *Papi* insists you stay. I am not a well man."

Thinking he was joking, Millie chuckled. "Right." But his expression said it all. It wasn't a joke. She clasped his hands and leaned toward him. "What are you keeping from me, *Papi*? What should I know?" She looked at Lonny and Mrs. Medina, her insides roiling with worry. "What?"

Mr. Medina pulled his hands free. "They call it cancer."

"Cancer?" She steadied herself with a hand to the sofa, looking to Lonny for confirmation. He nodded.

"It's okay. I'm an old man. I've lived a good life." He gave her hand a squeeze. "Now, help me to the bedroom. I'm tired."

Lonny hurried to his father's side. "Here. Let me help you."

He swatted Lonny away. "I've asked my sweet *Hija*. You stay here and help your mother."

Millie helped him into his bedroom and he sat on the bed. "Here, let me get your shoes." She knelt and pulled off his shoes and socks.

He pointed toward the dresser. "I need to take my pills."

Millie found them easily. They were separated by day and time. "I have them, but you need some water."

"It's here by the bed." He reached down and grabbed the water bottle.

Millie emptied the pills marked Sunday PM into a little cup and handed it to *Papi*. He swallowed them and grabbed his pajama bottoms. "Turn around *Hija* and give an old man his privacy."

When he was dressed for bed, he called for her to sit beside him.

"I'm so sorry," she said. "I didn't know."

"There's nothing for you to be sorry for. I have learned a lot about life and regrets, and I want to know something."

"What, *Papi*. Anything." She clasped his hands and patted them.

"You were too young to be so serious with my Lonny when you moved away, but we still thought you would keep in touch and marry him after college. Why did you send him away? Is there someone else?"

"No, *Papi*. I waited for him, but he never called." Millie blinked, but a tear still found its way down her cheek.

He scowled. "I should call your mama and talk to her."

"She's gone." The pain of Mama's death was still tender. Millie inhaled a deep breath and let it slowly out. "She died of cancer four years ago."

"When we meet in heaven, I will talk to her. It is not right what she did."

"What did she do?" As a teen, Millie had been so angry about leaving Lonny. "What?"

Mr. Medina waited a moment. "Fluff my pillow," he said. "I need to sit when I speak to you. I feel as though I'm already in my casket."

"*Papi!*" Millie's heart jumped into her throat. "Don't

talk like that." She stood and fluffed his pillow and grabbed another to put under him as well.

"That's much better. Thank you." Rather than sit straighter, he took the offered pillow, tucked it under his arms, then turned over and closed his eyes.

Millie waited a moment, thinking he would finish his conversation. *"Papi?"* She touched his shoulder and he patted her hand, but he didn't say anything. When he started breathing heavily, she left the room.

Lonny was in a chair, resting his head in his hands. He looked up when she entered the room, his expression unreadable. But he had to know what Papi was going to tell her. She wanted to know, too. *"Papi* was going to tell me something about Mama—something she did in Phoenix. Do you know anything about it?"

He got up. "Let's go out back and feed the cattle."

"Sounds good."

"Can I get you some supper?" Mrs. Medina asked.

"Thank you, Mama, but we might be a while," Lonny replied. "We'll warm up the leftovers when we get back." Lonny pulled a large coat from a rack near the back door. "Put this on. I don't want you catching cold. You didn't bring a good coat with you, did you."

"I don't own a warm coat." Her face heated, but she recovered quickly. "It isn't as though I can't afford one. I just don't need one in Phoenix." Because she never went anywhere.

He smirked and shook his head, and Millie wondered what he was thinking.

As they walked out and fed the animals, the silence screamed at Millie. Didn't he know what Papi was going to tell her? He had to, and Millie was anxious to hear what it was, but she knew better than to rush Lonny. He'd talk when he was ready. They flaked the hay and spread it out, then added enriched oats to the feeding trough.

"Do you still like walking?" He indicated the road with a nod.

"Sure." She hadn't walked for fun since moving to Phoenix, but he didn't need to know.

The dirt crunched beneath them, a sound that Millie loved. Several bats swooped and dove for bugs; watching this was a simple pleasure Millie had forgotten. The way the stars, by the millions, lit up the sky; filled her with awe. But after walking a few blocks with Lonny still not saying anything, Millie wouldn't wait any longer. Her emotions churned toward the surface like a volcano threatening to erupt if she didn't say something.

"So?" She crossed her arms over her stomach, tilting her head just a little, and looked at him. *"Papi* had something to tell me, about you— about us, and then he didn't say anything. He seems to think that you tried to come after me all those years ago."

They were near an open field and Lonny stopped. "It's been fourteen years. Don't you know?" He lifted his hands to her shoulders but then dropped them to his sides.

"Know what?" That came out harsher than intended, but she was tired of this stepping around the issue. "Mama told me that you didn't care about me." Her voice caught. "That you didn't love me." Millie held herself tighter, turning away. "You didn't call, and when I called, you never answered."

All of Lonny's emotions returned like a flashflood. "I did call. It was you who never answered. You didn't return my messages. I drove to your house in Phoenix, and your mom told me that you refused to see me." He gazed down at her. "Was that not true?"

"I never knew you came."

He should have trusted her better and he should have

tried harder. Unable to restrain himself, he pulled her tightly against him until he felt her heart thudding against him.

She unfolded her arms and slipped them around his waist. "After my father left, Mama was bitter for a long time," she whispered. "I don't think she ever got over the neighbors blaming her for the divorce."

He caressed her hair, then pulled away, looking into her eyes. What was she saying? Had she not refused him? "You never knew that I came."

"No. Mama gave me a new phone as a present for moving. One with a new, local number. If you called or texted I never knew. It all seems so sneaky now."

"I wonder if she changed your contact numbers somehow so you wouldn't be able to get through to me—or had me blocked." Lonny rested his cheek on the top of her head.

Millie sighed. "None of my old contact numbers worked, so I guess anything's possible."

"All those years of hurting and believing the worst." The defensive walls he'd put up began to crumble.

"Of believing Mama's lies—she did what she thought was best at the time. I can't doubt that."

But she had been wrong. Lonny wasn't sure how Millie would react, with both of them barely discovering the truth of their past—that neither had rejected the other. But remembering Papa's counsel about regrets, he pulled away and gazed into her eyes. He would regret letting her slip out of his life again, so he caressed her bottom lip with his thumb, feeling its softness, wanting more but unsure if he should try.

Her breath came in soft white puffs but she didn't move, her eyes bright and expectant. She didn't resist and his heart nearly leaped with joy at the prospect that she might still have feelings for him after all this time. He leaned forward, touching her nose with his and making a slight circular motion. Then he touched his lips softly to hers. It took total self control to stop, but he pulled away and satisfied himself with staring into her eyes.

Left with such longing, Millie touched her fingers to her lips, amazed that he could still affect her after all these years. Her defensiveness dropped like a landslide with her new knowledge and with his simple kiss. She wanted to be angry with Mama, but she had already spent much of her life angry with her, and with Lonny.

Without thinking of consequences, Millie lifted on her toes and brought her lips to his once more. Lonny embraced her tightly, enveloping her in a passionate response. For a moment, she lost track of time. All that existed was she and Lonny wrapped in a cocoon of emotion. Through their kiss she expressed her deep need and passion, feelings that she'd had growing up and that had been kept inside and waiting for this moment of release.

She still cared for Lonny. The thought hit her with a jolt, but she wasn't certain if it mattered. Millie pulled away and searched his eyes. They were different people now, with different goals. And Lonny was responsible for his ailing father. It wouldn't be wise to start something that would only break both of their hearts when she left for work. "I think we should go back," she whispered.

Without a word, they turned and started back. But just then, Millie got a strange premonition that crept up her neck. As she saw a faint vision of Emerson, the hair on her arms prickled. "Something's going on at the hotel," she said. It wasn't more than a couple of miles away; they had walked there as kids, but the mesquite and ironwood trees blocked the view and they couldn't walk there after dark. It would take too long.

"Let's get my truck." Lonny grabbed her hand and they ran toward his family home. "What did you hear?"

She placed her hand to her heart. "Nothing. I just have this feeling." Nothing like this had happened before— she wasn't psychic—her heart raced with panic. "I hope everything is okay."

When his truck was in sight, Millie released his hand and raced the last few yards, jumping into the passenger seat and fastening her seatbelt as Lonny started the engine.

Millie didn't know what to think or expect. If they didn't see anything, Lonny would think she'd made it up just to get out of their situation . . . but she had this feeling, like ants crawling all over her. Something was horribly wrong. "Can you go faster?" She knew he shouldn't speed, but they had to go all the way to the highway to get into the property with his truck. Lonny put his foot on the throttle and threw it into gear.

As they approached, Millie saw lights on in the barn. "Look!" She had seen lights the other night, too. The surrounding area was packed with cars. What was anyone doing in the barn? She thought of Anna's comment. "Do you think it's a bunch of teenagers, or is it someone looking for treasure?"

"I don't know." Lonny slowed and pulled off of the highway. "One of the deputies is already on it, though." He pointed to the sheriff's vehicle.

"That's a lot of cars for only one officer. Why don't you call it in, just in case." It would make her feel better. "That looks like Deputy Begay's vehicle, and he's supposed to be off tonight. It's weird that he'd be out here."

He stopped. "Deputy Begay? When did you talk to him?" He scowled, clenching his jaw.

Millie looked down at her hands. "He showed up at the restaurant today."

"You had lunch with him?" His voice rose in intensity.

"Well, yeah." She looked up, gauging his expression. "It wasn't pre-arranged or anything, though I think he may have gotten the wrong idea when we were at the fair." Her and her mouth. She waved her hand out. "It didn't mean anything."

"To you or to him? You said he got the wrong impression." He stared at her, grinding his jaw together, and hit 9-1-1 on his cell. "Yes, there's activity at the Ballard Hotel. It appears there's already a deputy on the scene. We just want to make sure he doesn't need any back-up." He listened for a while, then responded, "Oh, okay. Thanks."

"What did they say?"

"They said that under no circumstances are we to go out to the barn. Deputy Begay is the one out there. Dispatch called him on the radio, and he confirmed that he has everything under control. It must be a bunch of teenagers."

"Wow, it's exceptional that he would go out on his night off."

Lonny smirked. "Yeah, he's quite the man."

Millie nodded absently. Why did she feel this way if there was nothing wrong? Emerson was in distress, she knew it. "While we're out here, do you mind if we drive around the hotel? Just to make sure that everything is secure?" Maybe an intruder had parked in the back. The last thing she needed was someone going in and gutting the place just days before the sale went through.

It looked abandoned from the front. Lonny drove close to the hotel as they neared the barn. "It sounds like they're fighting out there." Millie chewed on her nail extensions.

"He said he had everything under control. I'll call again when we get back to the highway." Lonny pressed the gas and moved a little faster around the hotel, but a large backhoe near the cellar blocked their way. "What in the world? Did your company order that?"

"No. It seems like GK Investments is getting ahead of themselves. Either that or someone else is— I bet that's one of Kenny's." While the truck was stopped, Millie hopped out and ran to the cellar to see if the chain and lock were still secure. It looked as though someone had used the backhoe to rip them both off of the door. The action had ripped the hardware and the wooden plank on which they were attached from the wooden hatch. She stormed to the backhoe, climbed into it and pulled out the keys. Then, not knowing if that would stop them, she searched around the engine and found the electrical wires. They pulled loose as a unit. She brought them back to Lonny's truck.

She dangled the keys and the wiring. "They won't be using the backhoe until they talk to me."

"You know, Kenny could get pretty ticked at you messing with his equipment." Lonny shook his head and smirked. "He could call the sheriff."

"Let him. I'm in the right here." She couldn't believe his attitude. "I didn't do permanent damage. And he shouldn't be out here without talking to me and making sure the sale has gone through. And by the way, it hasn't."

He put the truck in reverse and steered his way back to the front, then turned the truck around.

Millie touched his arm. "I think I should stay the night here. Emerson needs me."

Eleven

Millie tapped her nails on her legs. "You don't need to take me back to your folks' place—I'll get my things tomorrow." She pulled out her phone. "Why don't you call the sheriff back and make sure Deputy Begay doesn't need assistance. I'll contact Anna Evans."

Her concern for the deputy annoyed Lonny. She had only been in town three nights and had already dated the guy twice. What irked Lonny was that he'd been chasing around town like a fool and looking for her Saturday afternoon when she had been at the fair with that jerk the whole time. Why would she even give that creep the time of day?

He clenched his jaw and called the sheriff's office again. He and Millie were getting along well enough, and Lonny wouldn't mess that up by being a jerk himself. The sheriff's department reconfirmed what he had suspected, that nothing had changed since his call ten minutes ago.

Millie put her phone away. "Anna said the backhoe is theirs. Apparently, Mr. Gerald Kappel ordered it, saying the sale would go through soon. They were asked to leave it parked in the back near the cellar entrance. Apparently he dug at the cellar without their knowledge. He just can't wait to tear apart a historic building."

"There's nothing going on in the barn." Lonny put his phone in his pocket. "I guess the kids thought they'd have an impromptu dance out there. What we heard was the stereo."

Millie nodded. "Sounds logical."

He did not want to leave her here with Deputy Begay— what if the creep came inside and had a sleepover with her? Lonny tamped down his jealousy. "I know you want to stay the night here, but there's nothing more you can do tonight and the deputy already has things under control." Lonny turned toward the highway and then stopped. "My folks'll be upset if you're not there in the morning. They've really missed you."

Millie looked back at the hotel worriedly, then nodded. "You're right, and I've missed them, too."

When he pulled onto the highway, Millie asked, "Can I ask you something?"

"Sure."

She chewed her bottom lip. "How long does *Papi* have? Or will he get better?"

That was a question Lonny didn't want to face, but he needed to be honest with her. "We're hoping for our own Christmas miracle." He stared out the windshield. "Pop has resigned himself that this will be our last Christmas together, although your being here has cheered him a lot. He may not last until spring." The honesty weighed on him. Pop would never get to see Lonny find love, get married, or give him some grand-babies. Pop would be gone before any of that happened.

Millie rested her hand on his shoulder. "I'm so sorry that he's ill. No one deserves a Christmas miracle more than *Papi*."

Lonny looked at her with a sad smile. It was nice to

have his anger and hurt toward Millie resolved. At least now when she went back to Phoenix, they could keep in touch. He pulled up to his folks' house and held the door for Millie. It was barely after eight, but as was their habit, both of his parents had gone to bed. Millie's stomach growled and Lonny smiled. "Let me get us something to eat. Mom'll be upset in the morning if she sees that we haven't."

"Well, we don't want to upset her." Millie followed him into the kitchen. "Besides, I'm starving."

"So I heard." Lonny chuckled as he pulled leftovers out of the fridge and set the containers on the counter. "Get the plates, will you?"

Millie got the plates and then scooped up some of the food. Lonny took her plate and warmed it in the microwave.

"It's nice to see Mom cooking like this again." Lonny heated his food.

"She has always cooked nice meals." Millie took her food to the table. "Did she quit?"

"With dad being sick, she tries to dote on him as much as possible. I tell her she is doing too much, to just stay with the simple things. She won't listen and then she's too tired to cook."

Lonny had lost touch with many of his friends during the time he was in college, and it was nice to visit with Millie. The conversation was easy and came naturally most of the time. After dinner though, Millie started behaving differently, more awkward. She touched her lips while pretending to consider something he said. The action was so unlike her. Either she was thinking about their kiss and wishing she could have another one or she was worried he might try to kiss her again. It was odd. He'd never seen her so rattled.

Millie stared toward the hallway. "I'd better get to bed. I've got a busy day tomorrow."

Okay, she was worried he'd kiss her again, but he

wouldn't let her off easy. "I get it, yeah. I mean, it's almost nine o'clock." He fake-yawned. "You need your beauty rest, especially if you plan on saving the ghost tomorrow."

"What do you mean, I need beauty rest?" She scowled, whacked him playfully with the sofa pillow, then came back to the kitchen and helped clean up their dishes. "You do have a point," she said as she dried her hands on a towel. "Considering Mr. Kappel's determination to destroy the hotel, it's more important than ever that we succeed in helping Emerson. I need to call my boss and let him know I won't be at work tomorrow. It's not like he's in the office on Sundays, but I do need to leave a message." She pulled out her phone and walked to the bedroom.

Twelve

The sun was barely on the horizon as Millie watched Lonny feed the cattle from the bedroom window. He'd been there so early that she wasn't positive he hadn't slept on the couch. It didn't matter. Remembering their kiss, as exquisite as it was, Millie was too chicken to go outside and help. She shouldn't have kissed him at all.

Could she just hide in the bedroom until Lonny left for the day? He stared at the window just then and motioned for her to join him. Great. Millie waved, embarrassed that she'd been caught staring at him. She left the window to get dressed. What had last night meant, anyway? Sure, the past hadn't happened the way either of them had thought. Sure, Lonny had kissed her, and sure, it was nice and the memory of it warmed her heart. Millie just didn't know how that was supposed to change anything.

When she came out of the bedroom, Mrs. Medina was in the kitchen humming and bustling around as though preparing for a party. "Did you sleep well, *Hija?*"

"I was very comfortable, thank you." She gave Mami a hug and kissed her cheek, then started for the back door.

"Can I get you a plate?"

"Thank you, but I can do it. In fact, let me get you some." Breakfast wasn't really Millie's thing, but she wouldn't upset Mami by refusing, so she turned back to the kitchen. "Go sit down and I'll bring you and Papi each a plate. It's the least I can do for your kindness."

"Nonsense." Mami waved the idea away.

"You are the only family I have left. Please let me serve you." Papi had always been more of a father figure to her than her own.

Mami and Papi sat at the table while Millie served them, then she prepared herself a plate so they could eat together. Not long after that, Lonny came in. While he washed, Millie got up and served Lonny breakfast, too. There wasn't anyone she was more willing to serve than these people, and Millie couldn't describe her peace.

The scene, even though Papi was ill, took her back to good moments in her childhood. So much so that she found herself humming a Christmas tune while cleaning the kitchen and putting the food away. Her cheerful mood held as she prepared to go to the Graham County Courthouse.

Her phone rang, and Millie looked to see who it was. Mr. Rumley. She was not ready to talk to him and ignored the call. If she discovered that the Ballards had children, finding an heir shouldn't take much longer. Maybe they would find the heir today. Nevertheless, her spirits deflated knowing that she would need to call her boss back and address her decision to stay.

Lonny insisted on coming with her to see the county records, and while Millie enjoyed his company more than she cared to admit, this had nothing to do with what she had actually hired him to accomplish. Did he expect to be paid? "You didn't have to come. Surely you have other work to do on a Monday morning," she said as they walked into the Graham County Courthouse.

"I have a flexible schedule today, and I'd like to know

what you find out." He acted so casual about it that Millie relaxed and went inside.

A middle-aged clerk greeted them at the counter. Her name-tag identified her as Ellen.

"Good morning, Ellen." Millie leaned against the counter. "We'd like to know more about Emerson Ballard of the Ballard Hotel in Solomon, and about any family he might have had."

Ellen looked surprised. "With all the hoopla over the Ballard Hotel and Bronco Bill's treasure, no one has ever asked about Emerson Ballard or if he had family."

"Hoopla?" Lonny's eyebrows scrunched. "Has someone else been in looking for information?"

"Oh, yes." Ellen's eyes brightened. "A little over a month ago a gentleman came in. He was curious about the legend and the treasure."

That was about the time when GK Investments had contacted them. "What did you tell him?" Millie asked.

"I told him that legend is just legend. The happenings were so long ago there's no way to prove it with facts."

Lonny drummed the counter with his fingertips. "Did he give his name?"

"An investor. A big shot from Phoenix, I'd guess."

Was it the person who hired Rumley & Riggs? "Did he leave a card?"

"You know, I think he did in the event that some new news mysteriously shows up." She rolled her eyes. "Let me find it." Ellen searched through the desk drawers and pulled out a navy-colored business card with the letters GK embossed in gold. "And look at this. He's been here before." She pulled out an older version of the same card. "This here's the proof."

Millie gasped, then took it and looked it over. "What do you think he's up to?" She showed it to Lonny.

"I don't know what he wanted before. I only noticed

the first card after he left the second one. He, like everyone else, wants to know where the treasure might be hidden. In the thirty years I've been working here, interest comes in spurts." Ellen shrugged. "I told him like I've told everyone else that's asked me: there's no proof of any treasure. After all, if Bronco Bill hid stolen loot in Solomonville somewhere near the hotel, why wouldn't he come back for it? And there's no record that he did. If Emerson Ballard won the stash in a cockfight, like some believe, it was probably hid at the hotel. At first, anyway."

Millie scrunched her eyebrows. "What do you mean by that?"

Ellen rested her arms on the counter. "I mean that around sixty years ago, a short man with bright red hair and a handlebar mustache came to town claiming to be Emerson Ballard's long lost relative. Even though he didn't look anything like the hotel's owner, his last name was Ballard. I've got the newspaper article if you're interested."

"That would be great."

"Okay. Let me pull it up." She got onto the computer and typed something, then turned the monitor so they could see a digital copy of the original. "He took possession of the hotel and started fixing it up, re-plumbing and updating the electrical and the like. Took almost a year from what it says here." She pointed to the screen. "If there was treasure in the hotel, he would have found it, don't you think? Would make more sense of his leaving than saying a ghost chased him out." She smiled wryly.

This was the man the Medinas remembered. Millie nodded as she and Lonny read through the article. "We understand that Mr. Ballard was married?" Her skin tingled. It was because of the ghost and had nothing to do with Lonny moving to stand right next to her, but she wouldn't look at him to confirm.

"I can tell you that much without any records." Ellen

beamed. "His wife's name was Samantha."

"Samantha." Millie liked that name. "We need to know more about Samantha Ballard, too. Did they have any children?"

"Let me see what I can find for you. Now, the birth records from Solomonville's early years are in the basement, if you'd like to follow me." She led the way to the elevator, making pleasant conversation on the way down.

"Ah, here we are," Ellen said as the elevator door opened. "You can wait right here while I search the microfiche and make a copy." She indicated a wooden bench.

They waited and they waited. Lonny sat next to Millie on that little bench, and his presence beside her grew with each second until his warmth crept up her arm. "This is ridiculous," she said, standing. "I'm sure you've got other things to do besides sit here. I know I do." She paced back and forth in front of the bench. Actually, finding the identity of a possible Ballard heir was her first priority. But still, sitting next to Lonny and pretending she didn't have feelings for him was difficult.

"Nah. Like I said, I knew it would take some time and I cleared my morning."

Millie made the mistake of looking at him then, and he was staring at her—her eyes, her lips—feeling herself blush, she turned away. What was his deal? They kiss once, and then—what? What did he expect of her? Millie closed her eyes and took a deep breath. There was no use in entertaining bad ideas. They would find the information Emerson needed to move on, and then she would go back home. And she would never see him again. Why did her stomach suddenly ache?

"Here we go." Ellen returned with a paper, studying it. "Samantha Ballard, mother. Emerson Alonzo Ballard, father." She showed them a copy of an old birth certificate and then placed it on the counter. "Samantha did have a child, and in December, too. But this other information is all smudged. I can't make out if it was a boy or girl."

"Does the certificate give a name?" Millie peered around Lonny's shoulder.

"That space is empty, but at least we know it was a live birth." Ellen pointed to the record. "We converted the oldest files to microfiche," she said, "but this looks like it was pretty weather-beaten before anyone got to it."

Millie looked over the paper. "Do you have any other information? Is there a way to find out if they stayed in the area after the birth or if they moved away?"

"I can tell you that." Ellen seemed proud of herself. "I happen to be a member of the Graham County Historical Society."

"Oh, nice," Lonny said.

"Emerson was shot and killed in the lobby of the hotel, and since Arizona wasn't a state yet, there wasn't a county cemetery. I'm pretty sure they buried him out by the barn somewhere."

"He was buried on the property?" Maybe that was why he hadn't moved on—he was just hanging around his grave.

"I'm pretty sure, and the anniversary of his death was the twelfth. He died on 12/12/10. It was a huge scandal at the time. That distant cousin came in the 1960s, I think. He went bankrupt, so that debunks the myth that he found any treasure. Two weeks before Christmas, he left without any forwarding address. It's too bad, too. The hotel's a lovely place, rich in history."

Millie tapped a finger to her mouth, thinking. "So he left on the anniversary of when Emerson was killed?" Either finding an heir wasn't Emerson's issue, or the man hadn't really been an heir

"I'd never thought of it that way, but yes." Ellen nodded thoughtfully. "The place has been up for sale a number of times, but something always happens. It's as if Mr. Ballard's ghost really does haunt the place." She smiled thinly.

"Yeah," Millie agreed. "Except I haven't had any issues and I'm staying at the hotel." That was highly exaggerated.

"Well, keep an eye out," Ellen cautioned. "There are all kinds of rumors going on about the place. I'm not sure it's entirely safe to stay out there."

"She'll be fine," Lonny interjected. "I'm staying there, too, to keep an eye out."

"Oh." Her eyes widened. "Oh!"

Millie smirked. That was the part of small-town life she didn't miss. Everyone knew everyone else's business— or at least they thought they did. They had hit the jackpot of information, but Millie needed one more question answered. "Do you happen to know if Samantha Ballard moved after Emerson died?"

Ellen rubbed her cheek. "I'm sure she did, but I don't remember anything factual, and there weren't that many options in those days. The historical society is having a meeting on Thursday afternoon. You should join us. I'll call the others and we can look for any information we have and bring it to the meeting." She brightened. "We'll focus our efforts on the Ballards and the old hotel. You know, I'm not sure why they don't put the hotel and the property on the historical register and have it renovated. But that costs money the county doesn't have, so I guess that answers that."

"Thank you, ma'am." Lonny tipped his head in acknowledgment. "It's time for us to let you get back to work."

Ellen straightened her shirt. "If you need anything else, feel free to come by. Otherwise I'll see you on Thursday. This has been a real pleasure. I don't get much occasion to talk about the Ballard Hotel and our fine history often enough."

"Thank you. You've been very helpful." Millie wrote down the information for the meeting and they left. She was excited about the knowledge they'd gained.

"I've got a bit of work to do." Lonny pulled his keys from his pocket. "I'll drop you off at the house and meet you there later today."

"I love your parents, but I'm not going to spend the day there doing nothing." He was being absurd. "I'll get my car and my things, and then I'm going over to the hotel. It'll be perfectly safe during the day." She gave him a sappy grin in hopes that all arguments were over. As soon as she got away from the Medinas', Millie went to the grocery store for a few things. After putting them away at the hotel, she would call her boss. She needed to beg forgiveness for not showing up to work today and to inform him that Kappel was overstepping his legal bounds. The man needed to back off.

When she arrived at the old hotel, Millie took a bag full of groceries to the kitchen, then carried her travel bag upstairs and set it inside a bedroom to keep it out of view. She went back down the stairs and stood in the middle of the lobby. "Emerson. Emerson Ballard. Are you here?" She waited several minutes in the shadowed room, but he didn't appear. If she didn't get out to the highway and call Mr. Rumley, he might have her termination papers drawn up. He didn't tolerate "No shows."

Thirteen

"It's a historical landmark." Millie paced the shoulder of the highway as she talked to Mr. Rumley. "Some locals think it should be on the register for historical buildings." Millie pulled the phone away from her ear. Yeah, she hadn't thought he'd appreciate that.

When Mr. Rumley asked about the heir, she pushed the phone back and responded with an exaggeration. "We're getting close to finding him. There's still more research we need to complete but—" Yes, she knew that GK Investments wanted possession of the property before New Year's. Yes, she knew their fee would fatten the whole company's wallets.

"But wait—" Yes, she realized that finding an heir was actually counterproductive to Rumley and Riggs' goal. No, they couldn't control whether or not they got a commission at that point. And yes, doing more than the legal requirement to find an heir, and then finding one, could end badly for her. "But I have something—"

"I've let you chase off on this fool's errand, but I need you back at the office. You've got more important projects to work on."

"I understand, sir." Millie took a calming breath. "But respectfully, I'm requesting my vacation days to stay until after Christmas. I've been reconnecting with family here, and—"

"I thought your mother was *dead.*"

"She is, thank you." Sheesh. "But I have other family here." She loved the Medinas like family, and she couldn't give up on Emerson yet. She had promised him a solution long before there was a commission involved.

"I'll do it, but I don't want to, and I'll be giving the Holder project to Alan."

"What! I've done all the work on that. All we need is Ms. Holder's signature." She hated living in Mom's old place and was counting on that commission to buy a condo at Tempe Town Lake.

"Ease up on finding an heir or I'll be giving your other main assignments away as well. If an heir hasn't come forward in a hundred years, he's not interested, and GK Investments is putting the pressure on me to hurry this deal through."

"That's what I've been trying to tell you." Millie leaned against her Miata for support. Her boss was agitated and this last bit could set him off even more. "Mr. Kappel rented a backhoe and has hidden it at the back of the hotel. It's illegal for him to do anything to the property until it's officially his."

"And who says that he isn't waiting? As I said, he's anxious to get on with his project. Don't interfere. Your job is at stake here. Do we understand each other?"

Millie's knees began to buckle and she pressed her hand firmly against her car. "Yes, sir." She hung up, trembling. This was just messed up. "Your job is at stake here," she mimicked, wiping at a tear. Mr. Rumley had been her boss for five years, and she thought she was his star employee.

Why did things always have to revolve around money? That wasn't the way people thought in small towns. As soon as she thought that, Millie knew her own truth: It didn't matter if she never lived here again, Solomon would always be home. "That really is messed up," she muttered, turning back to the hotel. Her mother was right, it wasn't wise to return. Now Millie had one foot in her old life and one foot in her new life in Phoenix. It was tearing her apart.

Lonny would probably be there soon. He always seemed available for her, like a puppy. It was kind of weird. Had he ever had any girlfriends—did he now? Finding the perfect someone was an accomplishment in a small community, but he might have someone special. She doubted it. They'd spent too much time together this weekend, plus . . . that kiss. He didn't have a girlfriend. It must be something else. Maybe Millie's perceived rejection of him had set him against relationships. It had for her.

When she saw his old truck coming down the highway, Millie felt a calm resolve. It was time to fill in that fourteen-year gap and to set Lonny free, to set them both free, and then regardless of her heart's desire, Millie would only stay as long as it took to also set Emerson Ballard free—if doing so was at all possible. Then she'd return to Phoenix. Her career depended on it.

Lonny slowed down after turning into the circle driveway. Millie was standing near her car as though it had broken down and she needed a tow. He knew she was probably talking to her boss, but he rolled down his window. "Ya want a ride?" He quirked a smile.

"Okay," Millie replied, and much to his amazement, she hurried around and got into his truck. That woman was constantly surprising him. He would surprise her, too. Lonny turned the truck and headed east on the highway.

"Say, I was thinking," she said. "Hey! Where are you going?" Millie buckled her seatbelt.

"I thought we could go out to the Gila Box. It's beautiful out there."

"Oh, okay." She raised her eyebrows. "You do remember it's December."

"Well, it won't be a winter wonderland; it is a desert after all. But who's to say that the desert can't be beautiful any time of year?" Any season with Millie Crump in it was extraordinary.

"Okay. Point taken. And it doesn't matter anyway, since we're not going for the scenery."

"This sounds good." Lonny briefly let go of the steering wheel to rub his hands together. "What do you have in mind?" He wiggled his eyebrows and grinned mischievously.

"Stop that." Her face turned a beautiful pink. "You know perfectly well what I meant."

"Do I?" Lonny loved bantering with her. He hadn't realized how much he'd missed the teasing. "Enlighten me."

"I was thinking that for as long as we've known each other, we don't really know each other very well—not as adults anyway. I thought we should fill in the gaps."

This was headed in a direction he liked. "So, you know I work two jobs. I own Gila Valley Property Managers LLC, and I also have a job teaching employment skills to handicapped adults." They jostled along the one-lane road as they visited.

"I didn't realize you worked with handicapped adults."

"Yep. And I have the cattle, but that's more of a hobby at this point—put money into it but don't get much out." He didn't know if she would understand, but while Millie was trying to save ghosts, Lonny dreamed of owning the Ballard property and using it to graze his cattle. "What else do you want to know?"

Lonny pulled up to a scenic stop with a ramada and picnic tables. They stayed in the truck, staring at the landscape while visiting and catching up for another hour. Come to find out, they had both attended Arizona State University simultaneously.

"You didn't go to U of A? You had your heart set on going there." Millie turned in her seat.

"And you didn't take environmental science like you'd dreamed."

"No. Mama insisted I take business." She dipped her eyebrows. "How did you know?"

Lonny lifted a shoulder. "It doesn't matter. I shouldn't have said anything." He stared ahead. What would she think if he dared tell her the truth?

"You took environmental science?" Millie placed a hand over her mouth, staring at him in disbelief.

Her expression said everything: she thought he was a loser. Lonny couldn't help but feel the sagging weight on his shoulders, but Pop was teaching him to live with no regrets, so he decided to tell her more. Then he would let this whole history, and their future, rest on her—and how she reacted. "I knew ASU was big, but I didn't realize it was too big to find someone."

Millie stared at him. Her expression was a mixture of amazement and letdown—as if she felt sorry for him for having loved her enough to follow her to ASU. Lonny couldn't stand that pitying expression. He opened the truck door and got out, the bile in his throat making him want to spit. He stepped to the railing separating the picnic area from the cliff.

Millie soon appeared beside him.

He kept his focus on the near-empty riverbed below. "Look, none of it matters now. I'm glad I went to ASU and I wouldn't trade my experiences there."

"So, you didn't become an engineer? That was all

you talked about." She walked over and sat on the picnic table. "Why didn't you stay true to who you are and to your dreams?"

"We don't always know our dream when we start our course." He joined her at the picnic table. "I got a degree as an environmental engineer. Graduated top of my class and landed a prestigious job with Greenleaf." All while hoping to see her on campus.

"You didn't! That had been *my* dream—you lived my dream?" The downturn of her eyebrows didn't indicate she was happy about it.

"I did." It had seemed like the best way to find her at the time, and then he had realized how much he loved it, so he'd kept his major.

"And now, nine years later you're back in Solomon." The corner of Millie's mouth pulled into a smirk. She gave him an appraising look, clearly assessing his reasoning. "They wouldn't fire you—did they?"

And there she is again, the new, I'm-better-than-everyone, Millie. "You say that like it's a bad thing, yeah. But it's not. The big city wasn't for me." He clenched his jaw and gazed into her eyes. He was proud of his choices.

"If your reasons are personal, you don't need to tell me."

As if she didn't know his reasons—did she have that short of a memory?

"Your dad." She put a reassuring hand to his shoulder.

"Yeah. Cancer. It's taken a lot from both of my folks." It had taken a lot from him, too. "Pop doesn't want anyone to know, but everyone knows. I help him get back and forth to his doctor appointments and help out when they need something. I came home last year, spent my savings paying off my school loans, buying my house, and starting my business." He heaved a slow breath. He hadn't intended to tell her any of that, but he hated that she kept judging him.

Her expression changed and he glimpsed the compassionate heart he had known in the woman she had become. "It's okay." She rubbed his shoulder as though wishing she could fix his problems.

He nearly crumbled from her gentle touch and the kindness in her eyes. His willpower was gone and he couldn't hold back. He straddled the bench and pulled her into a hug. "Mills, I missed you so much." He pressed his face to her hair and breathed the spicy scent of her.

"I've missed you, too." She leaned forward to kiss his cheek, but he turned and met her lips with his. His intensity took her by surprise. Millie planned to pull away. It was proper to pull away. To not kiss him. But he'd called her Mills, like he used to, and with such longing. She scooted closer, her hands on him, caressing his back and wanting to take away all his pain. His kiss was her lifeline, waking her from a fourteen-year slumber.

He pulled back, his forehead touching hers. "I guess that wasn't very professional, huh."

Professional? "Um, no." Millie scooted away, straightening her blouse. "I'm—that was my fault. Sorry." She gulped; she should know better. Lonny was merely upset with his father's ailment. He needed her support, but this would just lead to heartbreak. Millie was circling in Lonny's orbit and it hadn't even been a week.

"Um," he said, "did you find anything in the hotel—any papers?"

Millie wanted an encore to that kiss, but the spell had broken, and they were back to business. "If you can believe it, no. The afternoon seemed to get away from me. I bought a few groceries and stocked the hotel kitchen, then I went out back to see if they'd come for the backhoe." She didn't mention her unsuccessful attempt to contact

Emerson. "Apparently they haven't been back. I still have the electrical wiring and the keys, so doing premature damage to the hotel is no longer an option. And then I called my boss." She made a sour face.

"How did it go?" He put his hands to her arms as though wanting to pull her in for another kiss. That couldn't happen.

Millie stood up and paced near the picnic table. "He wants me to quit looking for an heir and to let Mr. Kappel do what he wants. I've interpreted that to mean that GK Investments can do what they want short of destroying the property." After that kiss, Millie could barely concentrate because she kept thinking very unprofessional thoughts. "We need to get back. I don't want to be stuck out here after dark."

The sun was already low on the horizon. Millie walked to the truck. Lonny got in and started the engine. As they drove back toward town, Millie thought of the kiss each time she looked at Lonny. In order to keep from touching his shoulder again, she replaced it with the thought of work and potentially losing her job.

"If there's an heir I'm sure we'll find him or her by Christmas." Millie wasn't sure of any such thing, but they had to for Emerson's sake. "I've got several other projects on my desk at work that Mr. Rumley is threatening to give to a coworker, so I can't stay longer, and I may need to leave earlier." There. She'd said it.

"Is work all you ever think about?" Lonny swiped the hair from his forehead. "Maybe there is no heir, or consider the idea that the heir doesn't want to be found." He appeared frustrated. "Or maybe he doesn't have the money to buy it. Property around here isn't cheap, you know. Maybe he isn't rich like your investor."

Had he hit his head on something? "An heir is the only option of possibly saving the hotel, and Emerson. If the heir doesn't want the property, or if there isn't one—then that's one thing. The least I can do is try." She would find the heir without him just like she'd done everything else in her adult life.

"Look, even though I live here, I have given up a lot of my plans—"

"Your plans?" Her voice rose. She took a breath and started again. "You don't have to help. I thought you wanted to." He could take his plans and shove them. Her coming back here had been a huge mistake. They were at a stop sign near the Medina's home; she pulled at the truck's door. A walk would help her clear her head.

Fourteen

Lonny pulled at her arm, desperate to keep her in his life, and to keep her in the truck until he parked. "That's not what I meant. Come on, you can wait to get out. I'm almost home." She shrugged away from him but stayed in the truck. "I just meant that, of course we will do everything we can, but it might not turn out how we always dreamed. Here we go." He pulled to the side of his parents' house. Instead of getting out, she sat in the car and looked as though she might burst into tears.

"I know you'll probably want to go inside and check on your parents," she said, "but I can't go in. I've got to get to the hotel while there's a little daylight left." She opened the truck door and stepped out, wiping at her eyes.

Lonny couldn't let her leave while she was upset. They never used to argue, and at this point in his life he couldn't deal with the extra stress. He opened his door and hurried toward her. "My parents will see you out here and they'll expect you to come in. Besides, I brought dinner today. There's tamales, frijoles, rice, carne asada, and fresh tortillas. It's in the house." He took a step closer and she didn't walk away.

Every part of him wanted to hold her close and convince her how he felt, but now wasn't the time. He satisfied himself with reaching out and carefully taking her hand. "Come on, let's make up." It had all been a misunderstanding, anyway. "Please, come in and say goodnight."

Millie glanced up into his eyes. Not knowing her place in Lonny's life or his place in hers, or where she stood with her job, it was confusing. His sincerity softened her heart. "I do want to say goodnight to *Papi* and to thank them both." She took several breaths to calm down before going in and facing Papi and Mami. Even though he was sick, Papi was a sly old toot and he'd know if something was wrong. Millie didn't want to mess up her relationship with them.

Inside the house, the Medinas greeted her warmly, and Millie's tension eased. At dinner, they talked and acted casual. Millie told them the information they'd learned about the Ballards. They were impressed. During their conversation, Millie itched to get to the hotel. The impression that something was wrong there, something that a quick drive around the building couldn't reveal, nagged at her.

"Dinner was wonderful. Thank you so much for including me." Millie scooted away from the table, stacked everyone's plates and took them to the kitchen. Lonny came in behind her, and they washed the dishes together. The tension between them returned.

Millie knew her being there was a burden on Lonny. He'd surely lost business. She was being selfish in monopolizing his time and needed to let him off the hook. "I know you talked about staying at the hotel with me, but there's no need. I'll be fine. I'm sure you have things of your own to accomplish." He had said as much, and she wouldn't have him feeling obligated. He was either having doubts about helping her, or he had business to take care of, and that was okay. He had enough on his plate with Papi.

"Not really. I've already checked on my house, taken in the mail, furnished dinner, eaten, and now I'm helping with the dishes." He grinned as though he was funny.

"Still," Millie faced him, her arms crossed, "I will be fine on my own." She heard herself saying the words even while remembering all that had transpired there. Even before she'd said it, she wanted to take it back. She wanted him to stay with her.

"As you wish." Lonny bowed dramatically, then turned and left the kitchen.

As I wish? Millie huffed. If he had wanted to be there with her, he could just say so. She put the dish towel on the sink and went into the living room. The Medinas were there, concern on their faces, but Lonny had placed her bags by the door. It made her heart hurt.

"It's getting late," Mami said. "We would like you to stay the night. You are welcome to, if you'd like."

"That's so kind of you, and I appreciate everything you've done for me, but there are things I need to discover that I can't unless I'm at the hotel." She gave Mami a hug. "Thank you for everything." She moved to Papi. "I will keep in touch, and I'll let you know before I leave town." She embraced her Papi and he held on with his frail grip.

"I am counting on you," he said. "You will figure all of this out and return to us."

Millie held on a little longer. "I love you, *Papi*," she whispered, and then hurried outside, blinking at her tears.

Snow clouds hung thick over Mt. Graham. Millie shuddered. Staying at the abandoned hotel alone was foolish, but she really did need to stay there. And she wouldn't impose on the Medinas another night. Although she enjoyed their company, Papi was sick. They didn't need another burden and neither did their son. Millie knew the stress of losing a parent. Lonny had reached his limit.

The barn was dark, the hotel was dark, and that was a blessing. Whoever had been there the night before was gone. It was a sign that she would be alright.

Unlike her first night there, Millie didn't go through the hotel and turn on all of the lights. She didn't want to draw attention to her being there. She did flip on the lobby light. An old box teeming with Christmas decorations was on the front desk. Lonny had been there sometime in the past couple of days. She gulped. Had she misinterpreted what he'd said?

The box indicated that he'd planned a nice afternoon of decorating. It was a glaring reminder of their disagreement, and she didn't even understand what it was about. That wasn't true—he'd suggested they were wasting their time. Millie had taken his comments to mean he didn't want to continue their search for an heir. The box hinted at something different.

Millie looked through the box, a feeling of regret chilling her. A car light flashed through the window. She tensed and hurried behind the counter, ducking. A crumpled paper lay on the floor. She picked it up. It was a note from Lonny briefly explaining his commitments for the day and asking if she'd like to go to the fair with him that afternoon. He must have written it Saturday. Her shoulders slumped. A fine mess she'd made of everything.

The front door opened. "Millie? Are you here?"

Feeling sheepish, Millie dropped the paper and straightened. "Deputy Begay—Len. What's up?"

"I was hoping you hadn't gone back to Phoenix yet. Is Lonny here?" He glanced around.

"No, I'm here alone."

"I'm not sure that's wise." He walked toward her.

When he got to the front counter, he placed his large, warm hands over hers. "I'm happy to stay with you—just as a safety precaution." He tipped his head. "I noticed the backhoe out back."

"I'll be fine." Millie slid her hands out from under his and walked around the counter to talk with him. "This place isn't that scary." And having him there would be awkward.

"Have you had dinner?" He lifted his eyebrows.

She sighed. "Yes, I ate with the Medinas." *And I'm only alone because I always wreck everything by coming to unfair conclusions.* That pattern had started when her father had left her. It had continued gaining strength as a negative personality trait through her mother's tutelage and her own misinformed conclusions.

"I suspected as much." He nodded. "That's why I brought dessert." He grinned and swooped his arm grandly. "This way, my lady." He took the lead into the dinning area and turned on the light. "Sit right here." He pulled a chair for her near the window and opened the curtain so she could look at the night sky. The table had been set with the hotel china and silverware. "I'll be right back." His cowboy boots clomped against the wood flooring as he went into the back and then returned. He placed a warm berry pie and a carton of ice cream on the table. "There's nothing that compliments a berry pie like peach ice cream," he said.

The smell of tart berries wafted to her nose, making Millie's mouth water. This was all unexpected but also sweet. Millie regarded his boyish enthusiasm as he served them each a slice of pie and then topped it with two scoops of ice cream. He was so different from the way she remembered, and Millie realized she had never really known him at all. She had judged him plenty without bothering to know the truth. "I'm sorry," she muttered.

"About what?" Len took the white napkin, shook it out, and placed it on his lap.

"About not being your friend in high school."

"I forgive you." He smiled warmly. "Make it up to me by giving me a chance. Don't get back with Lonny—he doesn't deserve you after letting you go without a fight. I would never have let you leave town." He traced circles on the back of her hand.

Millie pulled her hand away, straightening a lock of her hair. It hadn't been Lonny's choice. "That's kind of you to say, but we barely know each other and I'm not looking for a relationship."

"Just give us a chance. That's all I ask. If you like what you see, we can take turns visiting each other on the weekends."

He wanted an immediate answer, and it was awkward. "I'm not really in a place emotionally to consider anyone right now." She smiled apologetically.

"That's not a no?"

"It's not a yes." And it was kind of a no.

"But it's not a no." He smiled that wide toothy grin of his.

Millie thought his attentions were sweet, especially given their history. He'd gone to such efforts in her few days here, but she kept thinking of him as Leonard the Letch, and it made her feel guilty. She was a horrible person.

"I can work with that." He stroked her shoulder with the back of his fingers. "I'll wear you down. I swear I will," he said softly, then picked up her hand and placed a kiss there.

They finished their dessert and Millie felt like a school girl on a first date. It was awkward and sweet and unexpected. All in all, it was nice to have someone showering her with admiration, even if it was Len, and he also had a genuine interest in the hotel. He insisted on washing the dishes, but Millie stayed in the kitchen with him, visiting. He had played football in high school and told her a few of his favorite sports moments. His parents had divorced when he was ten. His father had spent time in prison. Len didn't disclose why and Millie wouldn't ask, but Len hadn't kept in contact with him.

"I think Mom said he moved to New Mexico, but I don't really remember."

"I'm so sorry." She touched her hand to his arm as a gesture of support. "A person should be able to depend on their father." Millie understood the heartache of an uninterested father. "We have that in common."

"We have a lot in common, and I'll prove it to you if you'll let me." He put the dish towel on the rack to dry and emptied the sink of water, then took her hand.

Millie tried to pull away, but he held firm. She tensed; there was no service out here if he refused to leave.

His shoulders slumped and he appeared defeated. "I'm not planning to take advantage. But hey, I get that it's hard to overcome my past regardless of how false the rumors were."

"I'm sorry! I'm so sorry! I just . . . we've had a lovely evening." She felt foolish that he discerned her thoughts.

"We have and I won't spoil it. My job is to make you change your mind—to consider me—not to do something that would get me arrested." He chuckled half-heartedly, but he kept hold of her hand as they walked silently toward the lobby. She didn't like it but she wasn't going to cause him more grief by overreacting.

Len turned off the dining room light and closed the door behind them. He had a mischievous glint in his eyes— Millie's pulse raced.

Just then, Emerson appeared near the front desk. "Welcome to the Ballard Hotel," he said, just as he had her first night there.

Len glanced at her questioningly. "It's Emerson Ballard," she murmured, backing against the glass dining room door.

Then, apparently noticing Len, Emerson said, "We've got cockfighting out in the barn for the gentleman."

Len's face turned white. "Cockfighting is illegal." He took a step back.

"I own this fine establishment." Emerson stepped closer.

"W-What are you saying? I-I-I'm a deputy sheriff." Len backed toward the door.

At Len's mention of being deputy sheriff, Emerson's eyes grew fiery with anger, his nostrils flaring. "You're nothing but a crook and a thief. Leave my establishment at once!" He roared the words. Millie flattened herself against the wall, hoping Emerson didn't notice her. She had never seen him angry before.

Len turned, and without saying goodbye, he ran from the hotel screaming.

Emerson shook a fist at him. "That's right you flea-bit varmint. And don't come back!"

Millie wasn't sure what to do, but holding completely still seemed like a really great idea. She waited and watched as Emerson greeted a few customers, unseen by her, and then disappeared. When he did, she turned and hurried up the stairs. She thought some on the events of the evening— and how Len had shot out of there without making sure she was safe. And Mama's words came back to her again: *Men's feelings are as fleeting as a tumbleweed in a windstorm.*

Later that night, Millie struggled in her sleep, pulling the comforter over her shoulder. *She was trapped in a square cage in the lobby and pushed against the bars. Emerson Ballard shouted from beside her, his ankles and wrists bound in chains. "Help me!" He moaned. She reached toward him but couldn't undo his lock.*

Lonny came into view. "I'll free you." He strode to the cage and kissed Millie through the bars. "Sorry, I've got other plans." He backed up and disappeared.

There was someone standing in the shadows, his grin wide like the Cheshire cat; Millie struggled to see him. As she struggled, Mr. Rumley and Mr. Kappel drove around the hotel in backhoes. "Leave the hotel this instant!" Their speed increased each time they drove past. "Get out now!"

Something rammed against the hotel, causing it to quake. As plaster fell from the ceiling, the walls teetered. She and Emerson were helpless to stop the disaster. A backhoe pushed through the adobe wall, its bucket pushing and tearing at the inside of the hotel. Dust billowed, and gold coins shot through the air like missiles.

Millie awoke with a start. The light of early dawn illuminated the window. What had awakened her? The hotel was quiet, but the gravel crunched outside—did a coyote howl? It had been a restless night. She wanted to lie back down and sleep some more, but the gravel crunched again. Her heart sped up. Someone was there. Pulling the comforter around her shoulders, Millie got out of bed and walked across the cold, wooden floor.

Fifteen

As Millie peeked into the pre-dawn darkness, her heart still pounding, she saw no cars, no sign of animal life, and the hotel was still standing. She put a hand to her heart and heaved a trembling sigh. It had just been a crazy dream caused by Emerson scaring Len away. It had been a good thing, though, because she didn't like Len being there. His expression previous to Emerson showing up had made her skin crawl. She couldn't trust herself enough to decide if the feeling had been real or if she'd been judging him on her past perceptions of him.

She padded across the hall and peeked through the window of the front-facing bedroom. Lonny's truck was leaving the circle drive and entering the highway. Millie pulled the covers tight around her. *What had he been doing here at this hour of the morning?* She watched for a moment longer and then, with the covers tightly around her, she went back to bed, hoping to get some sleep.

Morning was nearly over when Millie next arose. A quick and frigid shower woke her completely—even with updated plumbing the hotel's hot water was virtually nonexistent. Downstairs in the kitchen, she slathered a bagel with cream cheese in order to quiet her rumbling stomach. As she sat on the counter, she remembered the evening before. A faint hint of Deputy Begay's masculine cologne lingered in the kitchen, and her first thoughts were nice ones about his thoughtfulness in bringing dessert. Her second thoughts were more suspicious. Deputy Begay had been in this kitchen. He was familiar with it. He knew where the dishtowels were, and the china. How had he gotten in? Did the Sheriff's department have a key? Why would he say he hadn't been inside if he had?

She finished the bagel and jumped off the counter, scolding herself. Len had come in and prepared things before her arrival. Big deal. It wasn't like he'd come in and stolen her food. Millie checked the refrigerator and then scoffed at her distrust. Nevertheless, she kept her eyes open for signs of intrusion. Maybe he was using her to find the rumored treasure. She scoffed again. That was ridiculous. If there ever had been a treasure, it would have been found—and spent—long before now.

In the lobby, the box of ornaments was still on the front counter. She walked toward it, her apprehension building as she neared. The hairs on her neck prickled, and she stopped. The room came more into focus, like a camera lens. As she looked at the floor where she'd stopped, Millie reminded herself to breathe. A slight discoloration still tinged the wood, making her shudder. An innocent man had died in the same spot where she stood.

Standing over a murder site disturbed her—did Emerson want them to find his murderer? That was silly; everyone knew the deputy had shot him either because he'd wanted the money he'd won from Bronco Bill or because he had mistaken Emerson for the outlaw bandit. Rumors of a cache-full of loot and Emerson's involvement with an outlaw persisted, regardless of the fact that he had been absolved of being one of Bronco Bill's cohorts in crime.

Millie shuddered and then decided to try again. "Emerson, what do you need to move on?" They had hoped he needed to find his heir, but one had shown up sixty years ago and it hadn't made a difference.

He was still frustratingly absent even though the morning air was thick with his death, as though it had just happened, and she remembered his reenactment. A chill shot down her spine and panic rose in her chest. She needed to take herself away from this situation, for just a moment, before going on with her search.

Hurrying to the back door, she peered through the window. Dark clouds hung over Mt. Graham, threatening snow. The barn looked as though it hadn't been touched in eons, though she knew someone had been out there this past weekend. The weathered building showed its years, with dry wooden planks that didn't come together well enough to keep the wind out, and paint that had eroded from years of sun and wind beating upon it.

She opened the hotel door intent on breathing fresh air unmarred by Emerson's death. Pulling the comforter tightly around her as a defense against the frigid wind. She thought of Emerson and hoped she could find the location of his grave. Ellen said it would be out by the barn.

About halfway there, the hairs on her neck felt as though they were standing on edge, her skin charged with an unseen electrical current. "M-i-l-l-i-e," the wind whispered.

She put her hand over her heart and watched her surroundings. Once more everything appeared closer, zoomed in, and every detail within her notice. The barn looked benign, but as she took another step closer the hair rose on her arms. "Emerson? What do you want? How can I help you move on?" Her voice squeaked.

Millie walked forward, her feet weighing a ton, and each step labored. Through force of will, she got within several yards of the barn door. The area near the barn had fewer weeds and bushes verifying that it was a regular parking area. Maybe if Lonny came back, they'd go inside together— she couldn't believe he'd changed his mind about helping. Her coworkers always accused her of being cynical, but people constantly let her down. That wasn't cynical—it was realistic—for now, the place creeped her out.

Having changed her mind about walking the barn's perimeters, Millie turned to head back to the hotel. A county sheriff's vehicle pulled into the circle drive. Deputy Begay. The vehicle lurched to a stop. She hurried away from the creepy barn and toward Len. "You ran out of the hotel so fast last night, I didn't expect to see you again." The man was relentless.

Len jumped out and hurried to her. Grabbing her shoulders, he began scolding her. "I told you not to go out to the barn. You shouldn't be out there." His eyes held a wild expression. "It's too dangerous. I told you vagrants and escaped criminals use that barn as a hideout, and I'm constantly needing to go out there."

"If that's the case, why did you leave me here alone last night—with a ghost?" Millie shrugged away. "Sheesh, Deputy!" She rubbed her shoulders where his grip had pinched. "I'm fine. Thank you for asking. I'm out here to find Emerson Ballard's grave. Ellen at the county office said he was probably buried out by the barn." She glared at him, trying to regain her composure. "The place is too creepy. I didn't even get to it."

He sighed in relief. "Good. I wouldn't want any harm to come to you. It's not like you could phone for help if you needed rescuing." He grinned as though imagining himself as her rescuer. "Anyway, climb in. It's freezing out here and I brought us breakfast." He lifted a fast-food bag.

With no apology for running out on her last night,

and after that angry outburst, she wasn't nearly ready to forgive him. "I already ate and I have a ton of work to do today." She stepped away.

He frowned. "Come on. Give a guy a break. I was only worried for your safety, and this is only an egg muffin." He wiggled the bag as though tempting her.

She could see he didn't plan to leave unless he thought he was forgiven—she needed to treat him as she would a belligerent customer—make the motions of agreeing with him. "Okay." She opened the door and climbed in.

He handed her a wrapped egg muffin. "I have more if you want." He pulled two from the bag for himself. "I'm going to count this as a win." He took a big bite of his muffin, and grinned.

"What do you mean?"

"I made a vow to uphold the peace, and more recently to keep you from harm. I think that just happened. I saved you from going to the barn and possibly into a life-threatening situation."

Being near the barn had been creepy, but Millie hardly felt as though her life was in danger, and he hadn't given a thought to keeping her from harm last night. She merely smiled in response. Despite his attempt at charm, he was not dating material. She would play along while she was in town just to keep the peace.

When she'd finished her muffin, he offered her another.

"I really couldn't." She'd only eaten the one out of obligation. "I really do need to get to work. My time here is limited." And hopefully his was too.

"Can I help?" He rested his hand against the seat, his fingers brushing against her shoulder.

She readjusted her position so he wasn't touching her, and smiled. "You can take me around the barn. I'd like to see if Emerson is out there."

"I don't know." He made a face of distaste. "What's the

big deal about finding his grave?"

After all of his interest, she couldn't believe he was questioning her. "For one, I'll need to alert the potential buyers if there are human remains on the property. For two, I might like to dress up the grave and maybe put a marker out there for him." That probably wouldn't help him move on, but it would be a nice gesture.

"Fine. I'll take you around the backside of the barn and on the south side. He wouldn't be anywhere else. I've already been on the other sides chasing out riffraff."

"Deal." Millie didn't understand what the big deal was to walk the entire perimeter, but she could get Lonny to go out there with her again if she felt it necessary. As they walked around, Deputy Begay kept glancing around, his eyes shifting to the barn.

He was acting so nervous. "Emerson won't hurt you," she assured him.

"The ghost? Ha. Ha. I'm not afraid of a ghost. I'm just checking for rattlesnakes."

Yeah, except she was sure rattlesnakes hibernated in the winter. It didn't matter. They didn't find any sign of a grave, and they walked back to his SUV.

Len leaned against his vehicle. "Is there anything else I can do before getting back to work?"

"No. This is something I need to do alone. Otherwise we'd get to visiting too much and I'd never accomplish anything." And she didn't want him there.

"I'll take that as a compliment—and another win for Len Begay."

She told him goodbye, and he drove to the highway. Millie went into the hotel through the back door. The wind whooshed in and movement caught her eye. She bent down and picked up a chicken feather. "Weird," she mumbled, and locked the door behind her. She would look again for the grave another time.

It would be best to not prolong this visit to Solomon any longer than necessary. Not only had Lonny pulled her into his orbit with his familiar charm and passionate kisses, but now Len wanted to date her—but more importantly, there was something going on at the hotel besides Emerson's haunting. Staying had lost all its appeal, but Millie could not allow herself to appear weak. Mama always hated a weakling. So, unfortunately, she was staying in Solomon until Emerson was freed or the property was sold.

Sixteen

Millie leaned against the lobby's paneled wall, her heart thudding beneath her palm. She could not get carried away with her vivid imagination. It wasn't as though she was trapped in the hotel; she could leave any time she wanted. Her anxiety wasn't logical. She felt her pocket to make sure her keys were there, just in case, and went to work searching for clues regarding a possible heir. Maybe the man who had showed up years ago had been an impostor.

The drawers of the front desk were empty. She pulled on a narrow drawer to the side. It was either ornamental or stuck because it wouldn't budge. Millie stepped to the double doors behind the desk. They opened into the still-furnished living room of Emerson and Samantha Ballard's private suite. Old pictures hung on the wall: oil paintings of desert landscapes, one of the hotel, and a wedding photo of Emerson and Samantha. They were a handsome couple with a familiar look about them. Millie wiped the dust from the photo for a better look. Lonny clearly hadn't cleaned these rooms.

In her search for a filing cabinet or other place for

important papers, Millie opened another door. It led to a bedroom with an old iron bed similar to the ones upstairs, except more ornate. The head and foot boards had a swirling design on the inside of the rounded iron frame. The end tables at each side of the bed had small kerosene lamps. An armoire stood in the corner, and there was an attic hatch on the ceiling nearby; at the foot of the bed sat a chest with a rounded top.

It was weird being in the bedroom, as if she were an intruder. Regardless, Millie walked to the armoire prepared to systematically rummage through it. A gust of wind stormed around her, and her skin prickled. Dust and debris flew everywhere. "This is my home," a voice said. "Leave now."

Finally he showed up. "It's me, Millie Crump," she said, her heart beating wildly. She looked at the exit, prepared to run, but stayed put. He should help her, not be angry with her. "Remember me? I was a little girl. You comforted me when my father left. You told me your pain in losing your family." She had thought it was her imagination or a dream, but the experience of hearing a voice with no body returned vividly. As a girl, she'd thought he was playing with her.

The whirlwind settled and the bodily form of Emerson appeared before her. He wore the same blue paisley shirt, with an old and battered cowboy hat.

Millie jumped back, startled. This was him! She immediately calmed. If he'd wanted to hurt her, he would have done so on her first night in the hotel.

"I missed every speck of my child's life." His voice held the tone of deep regret, his expression was pained. Millie wished that she could comfort him somehow.

She couldn't change his past, but she could let him know how instrumental he was to hers. "You helped me through a difficult time. I felt lost as a child and you helped me. You gave me comfort and helped me realize everything would work out. Now I've come to help you find peace. Do you know why you're still here—why you haven't moved on?"

He put a hand to his mouth, rubbing his whiskered face. "I was angry, and unduly so. My wife, Samantha, had a gift with people. That's why I built this hotel for her. She wanted it, and I knew she could make it thrive." He nodded thoughtfully, his eyes sad. "To pay off my debt to the bank, I started a cockfighting ring in the barn. A gentleman liked to come around, a decent-looking chap who loved to bet on the cocks. Samantha didn't like him. Said he was trouble and didn't want him hanging around." He paced the room but his boots made no sound against the wooden floor. "What self-respecting man lets his filly boss him around? I should have listened to her, but I encouraged him. I let him stay at the hotel and gladly took his money when he lost a fight. By the time I learned the man was an outlaw, I had already earned a death sentence by winning most of his stolen loot. I was a crook by association. I won't rest until my name is exonerated in my family's eyes and my child lives here at the hotel."

Millie hemmed uneasily. Didn't he know that was impossible? "That was over a hundred years ago," she said carefully. "Your child won't still be alive." She wasn't certain yet if his child had had children of his or her own. If not, knowing would need to be enough.

Emerson scowled. "Only my true relation would love this place the way Samantha and I did. That is my earnest desire. I built the hotel as an inheritance, a legacy."

"But what about the man who came years ago? He was your relation." He said he was.

"Impostor! The man was a liar and a thief. Do you see one red hair on my head?" He pulled his hat into his hands. His hair was straight and nearly black; his eyes a deep brown.

Millie shook her head. No wonder the man hadn't succeeded.

"It pesters my every conscious moment, and I won't allow anyone else to take over my hotel."

She didn't want to scare him away before getting information, but he had to know. "You won't have a choice. We have a buyer who wants to come in and tear down your home." Surely he couldn't haunt without the hotel. "I need to know where to look. Do you know where your wife and child lived after you died?"

"I won't allow my home to be torn down!" Emerson vanished without answering her question.

"Did you have a son or a daughter?" Millie called into the air, unsure if he even knew. He didn't return or answer. Millie opened the armoire and looked through the bottom drawer. It was empty. "Maybe there's something in here," she said aloud, thinking he may still be in the room.

Millie knelt in front of the chest. As she pushed the lid back, the hinges creaked. In the bottom was a small assortment of old papers and antique photos. Millie pulled out a handful. The papers didn't appear useful—old receipts and bank notes. Tossing them aside, she looked through the old photos.

An increased feeling of anticipation tickled at her heart. She recognized the face in the photos! They were not the same person, of course, but the same dark, laughing eyes and a similar build with the same black hair. "Why haven't I noticed the resemblance before?" Well, how could she have? She hadn't remembered meeting Emerson until now. So much of her childhood had been tucked away as memories too painful to recall.

"I think I'll go up to the attic and see if I can find anything there," Millie announced in case Emerson was listening.

Millie pulled down the attic ladder, testing it to ensure it was sound. With her flashlight in hand she climbed up, dust tickling her nose as she entered. It wasn't a huge space, probably the size of the Ballard living quarters. As her eyes adjusted to the dimness, light coming from across the attic illuminated a cradle with an angelic glow. She touched the wood, dry with age, and felt a twinge of regret for Emerson.

The window had been painted over and matched the color of the adobe building from the outside so well that Millie hadn't even realized there was an attic or a window until seeing the latch. It had probably been painted to keep both the heat and intruders out.

Lighting the way with her flashlight, she peered through the cracked paint. The window faced the northwest side of the hotel and appeared to be a straight drop down.

Millie tried to open the window latches to get a better view, but they were stuck with paint. She shined her flashlight around the musty attic until she saw an old metal tool of some sort and picked it up. Whacking it against the latches, she was eventually able to twist them open. Pushing against the frame finally budged the window and a whoosh of cold winter air blew in. "Whoa, that's freezing!" She quickly looked out and saw that the hotel blocked the front where her car was parked, but a side of the circle drive was within her view. She pushed the window shut, latched it, and turned back to her task.

On the row of shelves sat several boxes. She pulled one from the bottom shelf onto the floor and blinked at the contents. An old cowboy hat. "Emerson, was this the hat that got you shot?" Millie took it from the box and looked it over with a feeling of reverence. "This belongs in a museum." Underneath the hat were several tailored shirts and jeans. They were still in decent shape for as old as they were.

The items, and especially the hat, made Emerson even more real to her. She couldn't let them tear down his hotel. It was part of her life, her memories, and a part of local history. Emerson Ballard was an actual person, and he had been wronged. Millie stared at the box's contents, trying to absorb the intensity of her emotions. Emerson Ballard was her family. Even though he wasn't related by blood, he was related through an unknown connection, and a feeling of love she had always felt for him. She couldn't let him down again. It was her destiny to help.

A car door closed. "Lonny?" Millie hoped it wasn't the deputy again. Her watch read two-forty-five, so it could be Lonny. Another car door closed. It definitely wasn't Lonny, and no one else had a legitimate reason for being there. The hair on her neck prickled. The hotel door opened and closed. Whoever had come in couldn't know where she was. What would they do if they found her? Millie hid behind the cradle.

"What's that woman still doing here? I thought I made it clear to Rumley that she was to quit snooping around."

That was Kappel. She recognized his voice. Suddenly, Millie felt more angry than afraid. He had no right being there, and how'd he get inside? The doors were locked. She climbed silently down the ladder and hurried into the foyer, quickly formulating a strategy for dealing with them.

"What are you doing here?" a tall man in his late forties said.

Millie closed the suite door behind her. "I was going to ask you the same thing." She stood taller, hopefully appearing confident and intimidating. "You came right in as though you own the place, and yet I know for a fact that no ownership has currently been declared." She squared her shoulders and looked him in the eye.

"I'm Gerald Kappel, owner of GK Investments." He spoke as though she ought to be impressed. He then pointed to the balding man beside him. "This is my associate, Kyle Allen. We're here to insist you leave the property. If need be, we'll get the police to escort you out."

"I'm Millie Crump. We've talked on the phone." She folded her arms.

"I thought your boss made it clear that you weren't to keep looking for the heir."

Ah, this was their game. They were bullies. "He did in fact inform me, and I am not currently here looking for the heir." She was now fairly certain she had discovered the heir's identity. "There have been vandals on the property. Unless that has been you—but surely you wouldn't try to make adjustments to the hotel or remove items before you have a legal right to possession." She gave them a pointed gaze.

Kappel scowled. Mr. Allen glanced away.

"Otherwise, I've been keeping a watch on your investment. I am seeing that any loose ends are taken care of so that your sale can go through smoothly on the twenty-seventh of December." She clenched her jaw, readying for their rebuttal.

Kappel thrust his pointed finger toward the front door. "I want you out of this hotel now."

"Oh, I will be out. Do you think rooming with a ghost has been easy?" She glared from Kappel to Allen. "I'll tell you it has not. I'm likely to sue for the duress it has caused me. But I will not bow to intimidation and I will not do less than a perfect job. When," or if, "you take possession on the twenty-seventh, you will be assured that the property is in pristine condition, and that no one will come seeking rightful ownership of what should be theirs. Due diligence, Mr. Kappel, Mr. Allen."

Millie walked to the door and opened it, indicating their immediate departure with a sweep of her hand. "Now, good day to you both. I have affairs to attend to in Safford.

Since you have no legal reason to be here. You need to leave." Millie's insides shook. She had never talked like that to anyone before, let alone a wealthy client. Nevertheless, she held their gaze until they acquiesced and left the hotel.

She followed them out. "I must request that you relinquish your keys. I will see that both sets are given to Gila Valley Property Managers this morning. I might request they reset the locks." She paused for effect. "Hopefully, that won't be necessary since there are so few days between now and the twenty-seventh." She held her hand out. "If it is necessary, the bill will be sent to your office."

Kappel pulled a key from his pocket and thrust it into her hand. "You haven't heard the last of me." They marched to the black Jaguar, and then drove away.

Millie watched them leave, her heart pounding, then shook as though she had lost everything. And in fact, she probably had. What had she been thinking, kicking Gerald Kappel off his prospective property? When she felt steady enough to walk, Millie went inside, straightened the bedroom she had stayed in, and gathered her things. She took them downstairs and put them in her car even though she had no intention of leaving right away.

Seventeen

"*Ballard Killed in Shootout!*" Millie sat on the attic floor amongst the dust and debris, reading the headlines of the old newspaper she'd discovered. "Emerson Alonzo Ballard, owner of the hotel in Solomonville, Arizona, and long suspected of being in partnership with well-known outlaw William Walters, best known as Bronco Bill, was shot and killed in the lobby of his own hotel last night.

"Mrs. Emerson Ballard, who was in their bedroom giving birth, was later questioned. 'I didn't know about my husband's involvement with any outlaws,' she said. Mrs. Ballard remains adamant on her husband's innocence but admits to having a quarrel over one of the frequent guests to the hotel. He was later identified as none other than the aforementioned Bronco Bill. 'The man made me right uneasy,' she is quoted as saying.

"The Ballard hotel, a place known for its luxurious baths, comfortable beds, and decadent meals, was also famous for cockfights and the rowdy crowd that gathered in the barn there each weekend. The shooting by Deputy Sheriff Buster Jones is under investigation but appears to be justified and merely an unfortunate case of mistaken identity. 'Mr. Ballard was wearing Bronco Bill's hat,' said Deputy Jones. 'I demanded that he give himself up in the name of the law. When he pulled for his gun, I had no choice but to fire.'"

"It's lies, all of it!" Emerson appeared, pacing the attic.

Millie gasped. "Can you tell me what really happened?" she asked, standing up.

"I didn't draw for my gun. Buster was on the take—had to be—else he wouldn't have been so quick with the trigger."

"Do you have any facts?" Opinion wasn't much to go on.

"The fact is—" He sounded angry, and Millie backed toward the window. "I was not in partnership with that lowlife. The fact is, I was not reaching for my gun. I was reaching for the damned hat—Bronco Bill's hat—to give to the deputy." He reached up. Jerking the ghost-hat from his head, he threw it into the air. "I want to be rid of this stain, and this hat, forever!"

The floor trembled and Emerson disappeared. Or was Millie trembling? She put an unsteady hand to her chest, trying to calm down. *It is my destiny to help Emerson.* She needed to be strong, but she also needed to talk to Lonny, to share her day with him. He needed to see those pictures, but he had been there that morning and hadn't bothered to talk to her. What could she say that would make a difference?

Settling herself back onto the attic floor, Millie searched the rest of the newspapers for clues. *"Deputy Points Finger at Bronco Bill,"* was next. *"Ballard Hotel Abandoned."* It was all very unfortunate and sad. *"Activity at Ballard Hotel Suspect."* Millie read more of that one. It was about Emerson's first ghost sighting the year after his death. She put the papers back in the box and shelved the boxes she

119

had gotten down. The contents of the other boxes needed sorting through, but for now, Millie had an idea on how to make up with Lonny. She would cook him dinner. She hurried down the ladder, grabbed her bag and left to the grocery store for something special.

An hour later and while cooking dinner, Millie thought again of the supposed treasure, or rather the stolen loot that Emerson had apparently won. As Ellen had said, it had probably been in the hotel at one time. However, if it was found, it was still stolen money. The bank would want it back. She smiled. Returning the money would lift Emerson's stain, and they might offer a reward for its return.

The reward, if there was one, had been gaining interest for over a hundred years. That was a lot of 'ifs,' though, and Millie needed to quit getting caught up in legend and start working harder to figure out how to get Emerson Ballard that eternal peace he longed for. Kappel would insist that she move out, even though escrow wouldn't close until December twenty-seventh. That was less than a week away. She needed to hurry.

Rather than go out to the highway and call Lonny, Millie decided to take the whole meal to the Medinas. She went into the Ballard suite and grabbed two photos from the trunk that most closely resembled Lonny and stuck them into her bag, then took her chili and cornbread out to her car. Hopefully, Lonny would change his mind about helping her when she told him how much information she had gained in just one day.

As Millie drove along the circle drive, Lonny's old truck turned off the highway and approached. A smile lifted her lips. He had come. She pulled over, then rolled her window down to wait for him. He pulled up beside her, his window down.

"I made dinner," she said. "Chili and cornbread.

Thought I'd bring it over to share with you and your folks."

Lonny visibly released his tension. "Sounds delicious, and I'm starving." Rather than do anything, he sat there, appearing to have a silent argument with himself.

"Do you want to get in or follow me there?" *Why was he acting so strange?* Had he not forgiven her yet?

"I'll take my truck."

Millie rolled her window up and pulled onto the highway, heading to the Medina's. After they arrived, Lonny helped her with the pot of chili, and she noticed that he was sure not to get too close. There was something bugging him. Her. But she hoped to rectify that with her dinner— and information.

While they ate, Millie pulled the pictures from her bag. "Look what I found at the hotel." She showed them to Papi. "Do they look like someone you know?"

"They look like me," he said. "But these are too old and I don't know that woman." He pointed to a woman that Millie assumed was Emerson's mother.

"They probably do look like you, but I remember Lonny looking like that at a similar age."

"Look at these." He showed one to Mami. She looked it over and passed it to their son. Lonny puckered his lips to the side, contemplating the picture, then said, "I don't think so. That could be anybody with dark hair. Besides, our family moved here from El Paso."

"Maybe Samantha Ballard moved." Millie took the picture and showed him the other ones. "Don't you think it looks like you as a kid?"

Lonny scratched his head. "I can see a slight resemblance, but I still say it could be anybody."

Millie glanced at the pictures again and then put them down, holding back her excitement. *"Papi,* I think that you and Lonny are the heirs to the Ballard hotel."

Papi choked on his cornbread. "What?"

Lonny's stern look didn't escape her observation. What was his deal? He should be excited.

Papi got up, shuffled to the bookshelf, and pulled out the family Bible. "We're not related to the Ballards or it would say so right here." He tapped on the cover, opened to the page of his ancestors, and pointed. "Mary Grace Simms married Jose Medina. And you see here, they're from El Paso, Texas." He put the Bible back on the shelf and returned to the dining area. "It doesn't matter anyway. What would we do with a decaying old hotel? I won't last long enough to celebrate Easter."

"We could start by paying off the thousands of dollars owed in property taxes." Lonny took a deep breath. "As if any of us needs one more thing to regret." He crossed his arms and looked away.

Millie didn't have a response to that. She couldn't mention a reward for treasure that no one knew existed. It was all a fable, and it had upset Papi. "I'm sorry, I was only trying to help." She gathered the bowls for the sink. "It's nearly time for me to leave."

"I'm going out to feed the cattle." Lonny headed to the back door.

"I'll help." Although he hadn't invited her, Millie followed after him. "I still think that as the heir you could put a stop to the demolition."

"You know that isn't true. Money talks, and we don't have any." He started the water for the trough.

"Well, at least we could try. It might delay the sale until we found the treasure or something." Millie couldn't give up on Emerson just because it upset Lonny.

He stepped closer, his warm hand on her arm, his face mere inches from hers. She fairly trembled with his nearness and the scent of his cologne. "If I was the heir and it made me incredibly rich," he lifted his eyebrows, "would it make a difference? Would I be good enough for you then?" He stepped back.

"That is so incredibly unfair!" She heaved an impatient breath and tried to calm herself. "We've been looking for Emerson's heir since we were kids. Pardon my excitement at thinking it could be you." She shoved a flake of hay into the feeder and turned, wiping at the blasted moisture in her eyes.

"Look, I'm sorry," he said. "It's just, I feel as though you're looking down your nose at me. You grew up two blocks from here but you act like a city girl." He added oats to the feeding bin. "Are you happy there?" he murmured.

"I *am* a city girl," she replied. "And yes, I'm happy." Would she be happy in Phoenix after spending this time with Lonny? "Location doesn't dictate happiness."

"Well, that's all that matters."

If her happiness was all that mattered, why didn't he just ask if she was happy? Period. "Look," she said, wanting to explain. "Mama worked herself into an early grave to provide me with a better life. And now I have one. I've been a city girl for longer. . ." Longer than she had been his girl. "I might have been too anxious to have your family be the heirs, but in a you-deserve-happiness way. Not at all in a get-money-so-you-can-be-as-good-as-me way. Sheesh, Lonny. I can't believe you think of me like that."

"Alonzo was a common name back then," Lonny said.

"I'm sure it was. But there are the pictures." Millie waved a dismissive hand. "Regardless, we'll find out more on Thursday at the Historical Society meeting." At least she hoped they would. "That is, if you're still coming to the meeting."

"Of course I'm coming. You can't just drop the bomb of thinking we're heirs to the hotel and then think I won't come to the meeting." He swiped his hair back. "Just don't get your hopes up that it'll change anything if we are."

Millie hadn't considered the likelihood of this story

ending in disappointment. She gulped, and blinked hard to stop her tears. It seemed probable that GK Investments would have their way by next week.

Lonny drew closer. "I'm sorry, yeah. The stress of Pop's condition is wearing on me." He took her hand in his. "I'd like to stay at the hotel tonight, too. That is if you don't mind."

Eighteen

"Ya know," Lonny said, "we might get more sleep and it might be safer if we stay upstairs. What do you think? Separate bedrooms, of course."

As if any other arrangement was an option. "I think you're right. Emerson seems to be most active at night, but maybe we can stay across the hall from each other—with the doors open?" Hopefully she'd sleep soundly enough that her weird dreams wouldn't be an issue.

Lonny nodded. "That works for me."

They went upstairs, choosing rooms with twin beds directly across the hall from each other. Millie pushed one of the old iron beds toward the doorway. "Come help me," she said.

"What are you doing?"

Millie smiled and shrugged. "Just give me enough room for the door to close."

They moved both of their beds to their separate doorways. It was a cozy arrangement that suited Millie. Then she heard a noise downstairs. "Someone's here." It sent a chill up her back that had her teeth chattering. "Did you hear it? Someone is in the hotel."

"Stay behind me," he said.

"I'm afraid," Millie admitted. They had no way to defend themselves against an intruder. "Maybe Mr. Kappel came back."

"What? He was here?"

That's right, she hadn't told him. "I'll explain later."

Together, they tiptoed down the hall. Millie clutched his arm when they neared the upstairs landing and started down the stairs. "What will we do?" she whispered.

Lonny didn't reply.

In nervous silence, they checked each of the downstairs doors to ensure they were locked.

Halfway back up the stairs, Millie saw a figure near the front desk, and gasped. It was Emerson! She pointed, but Lonny had already seen him. They stood at the railing and watched.

"The name's Emerson, darlin'. Welcome to the Ballard Hotel." He took a step forward. "I own the place."

He was staring toward the front door just like her first night there. She thought he'd been talking to her, but he was merely remembering. "What's he trying to show us?" Millie whispered.

"I don't know that he's trying to show us anything." Lonny set his warm palm to Millie's back and indicated the second floor. "You've already seen him do this. Let's go upstairs so we don't disturb him. You can tell me about Mr. Kappel."

"I want to ask him a question first." Millie stepped into the foyer. "Emerson. Do you know if you had a boy or a girl?"

His ghostly self swirled and disappeared without acknowledging her.

Millie turned toward Lonny. "I guess he doesn't like being disturbed while he's reliving his fateful night."

Together, they crept up the stairs. Millie hoped that Emerson would come back. She sat carefully on her bed. "I didn't want to say anything in front of your parents—I didn't want to worry them, but Mr. Kappel and his partner visited the hotel today."

Lonny sat beside her and took her hand. "Did he do anything? What did he say?"

"I was up in the attic when they came, but I hurried down and met them in the lobby. I think they believe the treasure is in the attic, but I didn't see it. Emerson's things are up there, though. And newspapers from when he was shot."

"Yeah?" He put his hands in his pockets. "I wish I'd have been there when Mr. Kappel showed up."

Millie ignored that macho-driven comment. "There's a cradle in the attic too. Before GK Investments takes over, I think all of their personal items should be donated to the museum in Safford. Seems like that's the least we can do for him. I'm sure there would be an interest." Millie yawned. She hadn't gotten much sleep the night before, and although she wanted to tell him more, she was exhausted and climbed under the covers. "Good night, Lonny," she muttered.

"Good night. Sleep tight."

His comment reminded her of their youth, and she fell asleep smiling.

A cold chill ran through her, awakening Millie with a start. The room was dark and still, but something seemed amiss. Her teeth chattered and she put on her faux-suede Chyla jacket, wishing again that she'd brought something more practical. She tip-toed into the hallway while trying to force down the lump that had lodged in her throat.

Lonny was on his stomach, his face smashed into the pillow, in a deep sleep. Millie stepped forward to touch his hair, but a noise came from outside. She couldn't tell which direction so she returned to her room. The front-facing window showed a calm night. Back across the hall she crept into Lonny's room and peeked out his window. A faint light shone in the barn, illuminating the vague outline of a vehicle.

Millie had to wonder if teens would really go out there in the middle of the week and at this hour. It seemed like something else. She started down the stairs to get a better look, but Emerson was in the lobby. Curiosity nibbled at her reasoning as she sat on the step to watch her ghost.

The grandfather clock chimed ten times. Emerson's eerie glow lit the area as he walked behind the counter. He spent a lot of time back there, enough time to hide a treasure. What was he hiding, and why couldn't she find it? Was it already gone?

Lonny came and sat beside her on the step. "What's going on? He getting shot again?" He wiped his hands over his face. "What time is it?"

"It's around ten. He's spending a lot of time behind the front desk."

"You've looked through the desk, though, right?"

"Yeah. It was empty." She would look again tomorrow, though. "Somebody's out in the barn again, too. It's just one vehicle as far as I can tell. Should we go out there?"

"Let's check it out from the back door," he said. "Since we have no cell service, it'll be safer." They walked to the door, staring out the window. "What do you think?"

"It looks like Deputy Begay's vehicle." They watched as a man got in the SUV and headed toward the highway. "I guess that settles that."

He walked them back to the bedrooms and pulled her to him. "Those beautiful blue eyes of yours need their rest." He held her close, his warmth an electric current she couldn't resist. He kissed one eyelid and then the other, then he leaned forward as though to kiss her lips. Every nerve in Millie's body tingled with the anticipation of his lips touching hers again. *Kiss me, please.* She gazed hopefully into his eyes, rising on her toes and waiting.

Lonny stood back, rubbed his hands down her arms and clasped his hands with hers as though he didn't want to leave, but the kiss never came and the moment was lost in a gulp of disappointment. He touched his forehead to hers, and whispered, "Good night, Millie Crump."

Good night phooey! How could he get her emotions all stirred up like that and then just walk away? She clenched her jaw to keep from saying something regrettable. In her bed, she punched her pillow, pretending to fluff it, but with more zeal than she would have done otherwise. Millie pulled the covers over her shoulder. Here she was just three feet from Lonny and desiring one passionate moment with him and he didn't act interested. Was she interested in Lonny that way, or was she merely remembering their past?

Nineteen

Lonny stepped quietly to Millie's bedroom doorway early the next morning. He wanted to run his fingers through her hair, longed to have her kiss him with the passion she'd shown earlier—just thinking about it kept him warm, but she'd had a fitful night and was finally sleeping peacefully. He wouldn't risk waking her just to leave for work, and duty called.

He had neglected his business to spend every possible moment with her in anticipation that each day might be their last. If he didn't have several day's worth of work to catch up on, Lonny wouldn't leave now. Unable to resist the urge, he kissed his fingers and touched them to her forehead. That would have to do. He turned and hurried down the stairs, checking his pockets for a piece of paper in order to leave a note.

Millie placed her nail extensions in her suitcase. One had fallen off, and she'd removed the others. They were impractical here. There was no point in reapplying them until she got back to Phoenix. Besides, being without all the frills of makeup and nails might put her in the early-settler mindset to help her find Emerson's grave. Millie gazed, unsure, in the mirror.

Less makeup was not a good look on her. But what did Emerson care? And Lonny was gone again without saying goodbye. That was just rude. But then, she wouldn't have been happy being woken up at dawn. What she needed to do was buy a notepad and pen for the front desk. That way he could communicate his plans before leaving in the mornings. Not that she would be there much longer.

She unlocked the back door and stepped outside, a gust of wind blowing dust on her. She brushed it off and glanced around. A few wispy clouds floated in the sky. She closed her eyes in an effort to concentrate. While the other day it seemed like Emerson's grave would be near the barn, this morning that didn't seem a likely place. Whether or not Emerson was disgraced in the town's eyes, Samantha wouldn't bury her husband near the barn.

Behind the hotel would be a more private and serene place for a family burial spot. Someplace near the old gazebo where she and Lonny had played as children. She stopped and stared in unbelief. It wasn't there. She glanced at the backhoe and also remembered Kappel nearly hitting it as he backed up. He had come back and destroyed it; Millie wanted to cry. Old wooden planks were scattered across the ground. Millie stepped into the mess in order to continue along the path on the other side.

As she walked to the center of the gazebo ruins, a strange sensation overcame her. She became a young girl of around ten. Her father had recently slapped her face and told her that she was a worthless piece of horse caca. She had run away, again. She ran to the gazebo and cried on the steps while contemplating what she would do or where she could go. Her father hated her. She was worthless. No one would want her. While engrossed in those gloomy thoughts, a gentleman sat beside her.

"That's all right, darlin'," he said. He didn't touch her or put his arms around her, but his presence felt like a hug.

Shame kept her from looking up at him, but he wore fancy cowboy boots. "Those look like rattlesnakes." He must be dangerous. She scooted away.

"These rattlesnakes can't hurt you no more. Yer safe here." He said he saw her there often and asked why she was so sad. She told him about her father and what had happened. He told her, "I'd give anything to have a daughter like you and to take care of her."

Not certain if he was telling the truth, Millie had peeked up hopeful that maybe she could go and live with him. "Can I be?" His chocolate eyes sparkled and he had a kind smile.

The vision left as quickly as it had come.

Millie wiped away the moisture on her cheeks. That moment had helped define her. It had given her a reason to stay, and she had met Lonny a week or so later. Even though she soon realized Emerson Ballard was a ghost and couldn't substitute as her father, that only made his regard for her seem that much more special; because to her knowledge, everyone else only knew him as a gust of wind or a glowing apparition.

He had come to her in human form during the worst moments of her young life and the gazebo had been their connection. Millie had vowed to help him after her seventh-grade essay, "How I'm Related to Emerson Ballard," had met an F from the teacher, the ridicule of her class, and a whipping from her father. Emerson had said, "All family isn't related by blood."

A large cottonwood tree was the path's destination. As Millie walked toward it, she looked through the creosote bushes and shin-dagger agave, hoping not to miss anything that could mark a grave along the way. She reached the shade of the aging cottonwood without noticing anything.

Millie ran her hand over the trunk. A heart shape had been carved into the tree fifteen years ago with the initials L and M. Lonny had carved it there for them when they had first declared their love. There was another, older, heart beside it and she knelt to get a better look. The initials E and S were inside of this heart. Millie now knew the initials were for Emerson and Samantha. Not too far off, the dry desert grass lifted in a slight mound. Millie's heart thumped. This could be it! She walked closer and saw the remains of what might be a simple wooden cross laying among the weeds. She knelt, turning the pieces over in her hands and pressing them against her heart.

"Emerson." As Millie muttered the name of the man she had wished was her father, a gentle dust devil swirled around her. "I won't give up this time," she promised.

Before the dust and weeds settled, she saw Kappel walking around to the back of the hotel. Millie tensed. Hoping he wouldn't see her, she moved carefully behind the tree trunk. He climbed into the seat of the backhoe. The jerk was planning to destroy the hotel! Then, realizing the key was missing, he swore and shouted at the hotel, "Ms. Crump, you will never hold a meaningful job again as long as I live!" He climbed down, shaking his fist at the hotel. "You're history!" He opened the hatch to the cellar and went inside.

"What's he up to, Emerson?" Millie whispered, not daring to move away from the tree trunk. The morning air was cold and she rubbed her arms. It wasn't long before Kappel climbed out of the cellar with a box. "He's stealing stuff," she said, although she didn't remember anything down there to steal. As soon as he turned the corner, Millie got up and crept toward the back of the hotel. She peeked around in time to see his black jaguar pulling onto the highway through a trail of dust and turning toward Safford.

After his car was out of sight, Millie turned to the cellar. The door barely covered the entrance and was weatherworn. She took hold of it, trying to keep away from splinters, and pushed it open. Natural lighting would have to do; her flashlight was upstairs. She walked down the wooden steps and stood in the center of the dirt floor. The wooden shelves that had held fresh produce and bottled goods in a long-ago era had been shoved toward the walls, and holes appeared every four feet or so. Millie wondered if he had found the treasure buried down there and taken it. There would be no getting it back if he had. Kappel was a sleazeball, and she tensed with anger. She stormed up the steps and closed the cellar door.

Wanting to feel safe again and to remember more of her past, Millie walked back to the gazebo remnants and stood in the center. With her hands clasped in front of her, she closed her eyes and tilted her head upward. She waited. But all she felt was cold. She scoffed and headed inside.

The problem of seeing Kappel nearly took away Millie's excitement of finding Emerson's grave and of reliving her special moments with him. Her first thought was to share her discoveries with Lonny, but he had been acting strange. She pressed her fingers to her lip, contemplating what to do. She went upstairs and got her bag. Locking the building, she hurried to her car and headed toward Safford.

The drive back to Solomon gave Lonny too much time to think—about Millie—about him—about what he wanted from life—and about the Ballard Hotel. He wouldn't admit it out loud, but the pictures did look a lot like him as a kid. But he couldn't imagine a future time when he would be able to afford a piece of property that large.

He hadn't considered his own needs and desires for a

long time. In truth, he wanted to spend every moment with Millie. He glanced at the bag of takeout he'd purchased from his favorite restaurant, and wanted to call her. He would invite her to lunch with him and his parents. He shook his head. That was lame. Besides, he didn't want to give his parents false hope. He and Millie were not an item as evidenced by her spending time with Len Begay. And she was a city girl; it was wrong to think she would ever be happy getting a last minute invitation to lunch, or anywhere.

He pulled into the driveway of his parents' home, heaved a breath, and pasted a smile on his face. He didn't want them to feel sorry for him or to feel guilty that they needed him so often. As far as they knew, his life was just the way he wanted it—not the lonely mess it actually was.

With the bags of food in hand, he burst through the kitchen door. "Is everyone hungry? I've got enough food here to feed an army." They didn't answer. His heart sank. Of course they weren't there waiting for lunch. Feeling lonelier than he'd felt the day Millie had moved away, he placed the food on the table and went to his father's bedroom, where he found them both napping.

Lonny nudged his father. "Hey, Pops, lunch is ready. I want you to get up and eat."

He opened his eyes. "Is our *Hija* here? I want her to come in."

Lonny brushed his irritation aside. "Pop, she isn't here. She has her own life. It's okay for her to live it once in a while." He braced Pop's arm and helped him to sit up and then to stand.

"Lonny, I am disappointed that you've become such a coward."

"Thanks for that opinion." Lonny gritted his teeth against further comment and crossed his arms over his chest.

"*Marido!* Husband! Silence your tongue with such talk!" Mom sat up. "Our Lonny is a good man. See how he holds his opinions to himself. It's his example that you should follow. Don't think you can say anything you want, because some days your words hold poison and I won't have you upsetting our son."

Pop shuffled to Mom and took her hand. He kissed it. "Usually, you are right, my love, but not in this. Lonny needs our *Hija*. Do you not see how he pines for her when she is absent?"

Mom helped him through the bedroom door. "She would be here if she could."

"This I know," he agreed. "That is why I also know your son did not invite her." He turned to Lonny, who walked behind them. "Be cautious in anything but love. You must be brave, *hijo*. You must cut open your heart and give it to her. Only then will she know how you feel." He coughed. The action seemed to buckle his knees.

Lonny rushed forward, bracing him. He wouldn't disagree with Pop, so he said, "Let's get you into the kitchen." Seeing his father who was once so strong, now weak and needing help—it tore at his heart. He didn't know if he had the strength left to do what Pop asked. He could not handle Millie's rejection.

Twenty

Lonny burst into the hotel wearing a Santa hat and carrying a Christmas tree. "I hope you don't mind—If you have other plans, I can come back. But I felt the place needed a tree so I brought mine."

"Yours?" Millie frowned. What was he doing? "You shouldn't have."

Lonny shook his head. "It doesn't matter. I'm never home and Christmas trees need to be enjoyed." He placed the tree in the parlor. "Will you help me put it in the stand?" He centered it in front of the window and Millie helped get the tree tightened into place.

"I had a lot of exciting and strange things happen today." Millie had wondered if she'd ever get to tell him. She pulled Christmas decorations from the box and set them on the counter while explaining her strange experience at the old gazebo ruins, and her finding Emerson's grave as well as the visit by Kappel. "It's as we suspected. Mr. Kappel thinks the treasure is here somewhere. He may have already found it. I've seen him carry boxes to his car twice. He cursed me and said he'll get Mr. Rumley to fire me. I'll probably have a message from him tomorrow." *Merry Christmas to me.*

"You should go back to Phoenix. Talk to your boss. He won't fire you." Lonny put the star on his Christmas tree. "I don't want you to go, of course, but you shouldn't lose your job over this."

Over what? Millie felt her insecurity over their situation take over. Did he want her to leave so he could get back to his normal life—is that why he hadn't kissed her again? Not that she should want him to kiss her. Millie looked worriedly at his concerned gaze. She had never considered before that he might be like her father. Millie shook her head at that random thought. Lonny being like her father was impossible. She had known him too many years to even entertain that notion. That was her mother talking, and she needed to quit letting Mama's thoughts poison her thinking. Millie wouldn't be able to love Lonny like she did if he were. Love him? Millie choked. The truth was there. Millie still loved Lonny, and not as an old friend. She glanced at him, worried that he'd somehow read her thoughts.

Lonny stopped decorating. "What? Are you okay?"

Millie walked to the parlor window and stared outside. She couldn't go around loving Lonny when he didn't return the sentiment. There were other reasons, too; she just couldn't think of them at the moment. Millie crossed her arms. "I'm thinking that I can't go back yet regardless of what Mr. Rumley does. I made a promise to Emerson and I intend to keep it." And once she left, she'd never return.

She had broken her promise to Mama about coming before knowing Mama had withheld the truth from her. Even so, being there was too confusing. If Lonny cared for her, why wouldn't he tell her? Instead, it was Papi throwing them together with Lonny apologizing. Maybe he was being nice to her to make his dad happy—last dying wish kind of thing—as she had done with her mom. Millie needed separation. They'd been seeing too much of each other— eating meals together—taking liberties with kissing each other—behaving as though they were a couple—that's where misunderstandings happened.

Millie turned and faced him. "I'm also thinking that you need to get back to your house and your life. You could lose your business over this. People are starting to talk. Just because I made a promise doesn't mean it needs to affect you." Millie had been on her own, without a man, for most of her life. She could do it again. She walked through the parlor, hugging tightly to her ribs, and stood in the lobby. Her heart hurt. She wanted Lonny to stay. She wanted to be more than friends.

Lonny followed behind her. "I don't know what I said—tell me what has upset you—" He stopped and put his hands in his pockets. "There is gossip, but it isn't about me."

"Oh? Why would anyone care enough to gossip about me?"

"Word all over town is that you and Deputy Begay—" He swallowed his distaste. "—are an item—I think he's the likely culprit for spreading the rumors."

Millie made a face showing her frustration. "I'm certain Deputy Begay isn't at fault. We're barely friends." She couldn't resist asking. "What did you hear?" Why would he think Len was spreading rumors?

Lonny shook his head. "I won't say, so don't ask." He chewed his bottom lip.

Yeah, Millie was done with this conversation. "I think it's time you leave."

"I don't want to leave you here alone. I won't. It's not safe."

That again. She had been there alone more than she'd had Lonny's so called protection. Millie clenched her teeth, steeling herself and her heart like she had after her father left. "I'd hate for the gossipers to get started on you too. Best get out while you can. Besides, I'm not your project or a child you need to keep safe. You might not want me here alone, but just remember, I don't need a babysitter or your permission."

"Yes, ma'am." Lonny's jaw set, and without looking her in the eye, he turned and left.

He had barely even put up a fight for her. Millie stood in the lobby, her bottom lip quivering, and stared at the door Lonny had left through. His headlights shone through the window as he turned and drove away.

What had she done? She had such high hopes for the evening and now Lonny was gone. There was no apologizing and getting him to come back; he probably hated her. And the fault was all hers. She kept letting Mama's voice into her head, and that was no way to find happiness. Grabbing the last few ornaments, she put them on the tree. "I didn't even want a stupid Christmas tree." Millie had only agreed because it seemed important to Lonny.

Afterward, Millie reclined on the divan in the semi-darkness. Maybe this was why she never had long term relationships—she always assumed the worst. It was what her colleagues always said. Now that she thought back on their conversation, Lonny was probably just trying to help. Whatever. It was too late now, and it was probably for the best. She hadn't wanted to stir up old feelings anyway, and it had only ended in heartache. Just like Mama had said it would. She scowled into the darkness.

Christmas was Sunday and Millie needed to get Emerson's dilemma figured out. She couldn't do that while Lonny was her focus. She had hoped Lonny was Emerson's descendant, but wouldn't Emerson recognize him as his heir? Wouldn't a ghost know his own descendant without having to be introduced as such? It was ridiculous.

It seemed even less likely that there was a treasure on the property. If there had ever been one, Kappel had already taken it. Millie had read up on Bronco Bill and confirmed he'd been released from prison before his death, and that there was no evidence he'd ever come back to Solomonville. But the voice in Millie's head reasoned, even if there had been a treasure and Bronco Bill had come back for it, he wouldn't have let anyone know. He'd have done it in secret. Millie fell asleep on the divan never bothering to get a blanket or to even go upstairs and change.

The grandfather clock struck ten. Millie awoke to the chill in the room, her teeth chattering. An eerie glow lit the foyer. Emerson. He spent a lot of time behind that counter, enough time to hide a treasure. Maybe it hadn't been buried in the cellar. What was he hiding, and why couldn't they find it—or was it already gone? He came from around the counter and strode toward her. Millie sucked in a breath, pushing herself back into the divan. He walked straight past her. She wanted to turn around and watch him, but she didn't dare move. It would break his spell as he remembered his death.

Although some of the details weren't the same as Ellen had explained them, it seemed that Emerson Ballard relived the same moment every year in the weeks before Christmas. Millie suspected he needed the heir to take over the hotel. It was a mystery, and one Millie needed to solve without the ghost's help.

After a brief moment, Emerson walked back to the foyer. Millie let her breath out, and then caught it again as he relived his murder. After he was gone, she waited to see if he'd come back and relive his last night again. When he didn't, Millie ran from the parlor and up the stairs to her room. After pushing the door closed and locking it, she jumped into bed and threw the covers over her head. What if someone saw her lone car out front and tried to break in?

Twenty-One

Millie arrived at the museum for the Historical Society meeting late Thursday afternoon. She hadn't seen Lonny since the night before and was nervous about whether or not he would show up. How would she react if he did, or how should she? She shouldn't have invited him to leave when she really wanted him to stay. She loved him and had chased him away. But the truth was, he left without a fight.

When Millie went inside, Ellen greeted her. "I'm so glad you came," she said. "I found more information regarding the Ballard Hotel, but I didn't know how to contact you." She looked around. "Where's your friend—is he coming?"

"I'm not sure, but probably not. He's been busy lately." Such lame excuses, but she wouldn't tell a stranger the details of her chasing him off. Just as her mother had done. "Let's go ahead, and if he comes, he comes. I'll fill him in later if he doesn't." She would have to do something big to make up with him.

"Come on in and meet the rest of our members." Ellen introduced Millie to several women and the few men in attendance. They were a lovely group of people—none seemed aware of any gossip regarding her, but most were about the Medinas' age. Maybe they weren't part of the same rumor mill that Lonny had apparently joined.

Millie left a vacant chair next to her in case Lonny came. He had said he would. They called their meeting to order, read minutes from their last meeting, stated the subject for their current meeting, and introduced Millie as their guest for the evening. As they welcomed her into the group and made her an honorary member, she glanced at the door, wishing Lonny would walk through it.

"You came on the right night," Ellen said. "It's our annual Christmas gift exchange. We'll have that and yummy desserts after the meeting. You're welcome to stay."

They had gathered information regarding Samantha Ballard, and piece by piece, the puzzle of Emerson Ballard's heir came together. Ellen took the floor, saying, "I did some research and discovered that Samantha Ballard did move. On January second, 1911, she left for El Paso, Texas."

Papi had said his grandmother was from El Paso. Millie sat straighter in her chair. Someone else requested to speak and said, "Samantha Ballard met and married a man by the name of Edward Simms." He lifted a copy of the document.

The name of Simms sounded familiar and Millie thought that might be Papi's grandmother's last name. She tingled with anticipation.

A different woman asked to speak. She said, "On a hunch, I contacted the agency that stores adoption records in that area. There's record that Edward Simms adopted a child by the name of Mary Grace Ballard, the daughter of Samantha Ballard Simms. They changed her last name to Simms.

"That's it!" Millie's excitement brought her to her feet.

As quickly as her excitement rose, it deflated when a previous comment of Lonny's entered her thoughts. *"Maybe the heir doesn't want to be found. Or maybe he doesn't have any interest in buying the hotel because maybe he isn't rich."* His frustration made more sense now. He had also felt that his family were the heirs, and it broke his heart that he couldn't afford the property.

"Thank you," Millie said, more subdued. "This is the information I was hoping for. I'm not sure there's anything else, but if you find more, call me." She wrote down her cell number. "Or leave a message. We don't get cell service at the hotel, but it'll go through once I reach the highway. Mary Grace links the Medinas in Solomon to the Ballard hotel. She grew up and married Jose Medina."

"That's correct." Ellen appeared curious as to how she knew that information. "They got married in El Paso."

"The man with me earlier in the week, Lonny Medina, is Emerson Ballard's great-great grandson." She couldn't keep the smile from her face.

"Oh, my." Ellen clapped her hands. "There is an heir and he lives right here? That's wonderful news! What an elegant ending to the hotel's history." The others joined her in clapping.

Elegant. Yes. But only if the Medinas could take ownership. It was time for Millie to go to the Medinas and apologize to Lonny. She waited impatiently until the meeting's end and once more greeted the members individually. "I would love to stay longer," she said, "but your gift of knowledge is the best gift you could have given me. Thank you. If you discover anything else, please call me." Millie left the courthouse feeling as happy as she'd been in a while, but then she realized that, although this information helped to prove she was right, it didn't help the Medinas' situation. They didn't have the money to care for the hotel.

Millie needed a Christmas miracle—a way for the Medinas to claim their rightful inheritance, and a way to put the Christmas ghost to his eternal rest. For the first time since she was a girl, Millie drove of her own accord to the small church in Solomon, the one she had attended as a girl. The same one she had gone to with Lonny and the Medinas the previous Sunday. She needed to pray for the desires in her heart. Her hands shook as she drew near. The phone rang. It was Mr. Rumley. She couldn't deal with him now. She clicked her phone off, parking near a familiar old truck. *Why is he here in the middle of the week?*

Millie stood outside for a time, too chicken to go in, and stared at the aging whitewashed structure. It had held her faith and sustained her for nearly sixteen years, but she hadn't prayed since leaving. Her overwhelming need to pray now weakened her knees and brought long-pent-up emotions to the surface. She wiped her eyes, staring toward the bell tower. "God, do you love me?" Millie hadn't loved Him. Hadn't even thought of Him for half her life, but standing there transformed her to the girl she had been, with braided pigtails wrapped around her head, and adorned with weed-blossoms. She put her hand on the old brassy doorknob.

Dare she go in? Would Lonny think she was merely following him? It was only a moment's hesitation. He would never discourage her prayers. Millie opened the door, standing inside until her eyes adjusted. She walked, trembling, to the bent figure in the second pew, and knelt beside him.

She felt awkward at first, not quite knowing what Lonny thought of her being there, or how to speak aloud the desires of her heart in front of him. But she knew that doing so was right. "Father, God, please forgive me of my many sins. Help me to be strong. Guide me in helping those I love to find their way home. This, I know I cannot do alone. I am weak and Thou, dear God, are strong. I need a miracle at Thy hand. Amen." Millie knew she wasn't worthy of a miracle. It was a bold request, but the prayer wasn't for her.

Lonny reached out and held her hand, taking it to his lips with a gentle kiss. Her heart erupted with love for this man beside her. He held the key to making her whole. She turned, caressing his cheek. It was moist. She tipped her head to his, waiting, hoping that he would trust her with his troubles.

"Pop's cancer isn't responding to treatment." He choked out the words and Millie took him into her embrace.

"I'm so sorry," she whispered. "I'm so sorry." She stroked his back and his hair, remembering her own mother's passing a few years prior. "You're not alone. I'm here."

His expression was haunted and full of pain. He pulled her close, his lips drawing across her cheek until meeting hers. His kiss was passionate and demanding, and full of the pain she knew he must feel. She returned his passion, a starving woman, slaked by the man she loved. He ended their kiss, sobbing. "I can't lose him."

Millie held him, stroking his hair and his back.

After a moment, she took both of Lonny's hands in hers and prayed for Mr. Medina and for his family's continued strength during this trial, asking that they would feel the Lord's comfort. As she prayed for Lonny, she felt an overwhelming peace envelop her. She stopped her prayer to gain control of her voice, then said, "Amen."

They knelt in silence as one unit, one couple, and it scared Millie to realize the depth of her feelings. She itched to break this connection, this influence Lonny had with her so that he couldn't hurt her the way her father had, but the Holy Spirit, and her own feelings, were stronger.

"Oh, Mills," he whispered, touching his forehead to hers, "I only want what's best for you."

She knew that and hugged him in response. "I'm sorry

I overreacted. I'd wanted the evening to be special." Millie then told him about the visit from GK Investments. "They ordered me out of the hotel. I ordered them out as well." She grinned. "I made them give me their key." She pulled it out and dangled it. Then, she remembered why Lonny was at the church. He was in pain. His father was ill and dying. In all their adventures, Millie had always been the instigator, but now she felt Lonny's need and handed him the hotel keys. "Let's forget about the hotel for now. What would you like to do? I'm here for you."

Twenty-Two

Mr. Medina looked more frail than Millie had ever seen him. She hoped he wasn't giving up. "Hey, *Papi.*" She pressed back the emotion in her voice. "I hear you're under the weather."

"Seeing your beautiful face has made my day." He reached out and Millie took his hands in hers.

"You're a flatterer," she said. "I should visit more often." As soon as she said it, Millie was afraid it was the wrong thing. What would they think of her bold statement?

"You should stick around. You're like my own daughter," Papi said. "Maybe daughter-in-law." He winked. "I know it's sure been nice to see my son happy again."

"Pop!" Lonny scolded, sitting on a chair beside the bed. "You know Millie has an important job in Phoenix."

"I do have some good news, though," Millie said. She sat on his bed. "Turns out that Samantha Ballard gave birth to a daughter. Her name was Mary Grace. Does that name sound familiar?" She glanced up at Lonny, hoping he wasn't upset, then continued. "After moving to El Paso, Samantha married Edward Simms and he adopted Mary

Grace. After she grew up, Mary Grace Simms married a man by the name of Jose Medina." Millie squeezed Papi's hand and then let go.

"Jose Medina was my grandfather." Papi clasped his covers, and the corners of his mouth lifted. "Just think, I knew Emerson Ballard's daughter, *mi abuela*." He reached for Lonny, who sat beside Millie. "The Ballard Hotel is ours. We should not let strangers tear it down."

Lonny shook his head, frowning. "Pop, we can't afford it."

"I know. I know." He patted Lonny's hand, then reached for Millie. "But that's almost everything I need to die a happy man." He coughed a deep, rattling cough. It worried Millie and she saw Lonny's worried expression. "Almost everything?" She would do anything for the Medinas.

"Marry my Lonny. He needs a good woman to keep him in line." He coughed again.

"Pop! Stop that!" Lonny paced the floor.

"Get well, Mr. Medina, and we'll talk about it." She smiled down at him.

"You quit giving these kids a hard time." Mrs. Medina came forward with a tray of food. "They got their whole life to live and don't need you butting in."

Millie stood out of the way while Lonny helped his father get situated, then took the tray from his mother and set it on Papi's lap. "We're going to go now so you can eat in peace. Be sure to eat it all." He gave his father a concerned look, turned and kissed his mother on the cheek. "You're a strong woman putting up with that stubborn man for all these years," he said with a smile.

"It's been my pleasure," Mrs. Medina said, her eyes teary. She put her fingers to her mouth and hurried from the room.

Mr. Medina took a bite of the sandwich. Lonny led Millie from the room and the door. They stood on the front patio, and he swiped his hand through his hair. "I'm sorry about that," he said.

"Don't worry about it." Millie waved her hand dismissively and sat on the front step. She thought it was cute. It pleased her that Papi thought she would make a good wife for his son. Her hope was that Lonny could feel the same.

"Do you want to go somewhere?" Lonny sagged down beside her. "We could do something. This sitting around is driving me crazy."

"My boss called earlier and I didn't pick up." She made a face to hide her worry over getting fired. "I need to call him back. We'll do something after that, okay?" When he nodded, she hit "redial."

Lonny went inside as Mr. Rumley answered.

He started right in, railing on her. "Gerald Kappel called. He told me that you're making yourself at home with the Solomon property. Said you've vandalized equipment he's placed there, and are doing everything in your power to stop the sale from going through. Tell me it isn't true. If it is, I have a mind to take his advice in firing you."

"It's not what you think. Mr. Kappel is exaggerating the situation. While it is true that I've stayed a few nights in the hotel—"

He cut her off with a string of profanities.

After that, Millie wasn't sure she wanted to keep her job. "Hear me out before you make your final decision." When he calmed down, she continued. "There has been a lot of activity out there, and the county sheriff's department is constantly involved. We've caught intruders there at all different times of the day, and even in the middle of the night." Several of those instances were from GK Investments, but she didn't mention that. "Now, I know what you said about staying away, but I don't think it's wise to leave the property unattended."

"It sounds dangerous. You should contact the police."

"We have, sir." Millie rolled her eyes. "The Sheriff's department has jurisdiction. We've been asked to keep an eye out and to go straight to the deputy sheriff if we see any more suspicious vehicles on the property."

"Why all the interest in the property now?"

"I don't know, but it could have something to do with the rumored treasure." She knew that was Kappel's reasoning. "Vacant properties are a popular place for illegal activities of all sorts."

"It does sound advisable to have someone on site to guard the place until the sale, but it's too dangerous for you. The property manager should do it. That's what we're paying him for."

"With all due respect, sir, we only paid him to make the place presentable and to make sure the plumbing and electric worked. His job is done."

"Tell him we'll pay him double-time if he'll guard the place at night until the twenty-seventh."

"That's a generous offer, but I'm not sure he can. He just found out his father's cancer treatments aren't working."

"Sounds like he'll need the money, then."

"Perhaps. If he can't, then you can count on me to guard the place."

"Ms. Crump, when I called, I had half a mind to let you go. The way that Gerald carried on, he made it sound as though you were taking all kinds of liberties with the hotel, but it sounds as though you have everything under control. I'll leave you to it. Oh, and by the way, Ms. Holder is out of town until after the New Year. You can close her contract when she gets back. Your other accounts are safe, too." He chuckled. "Have yourself a Merry Christmas, but be back as soon as you can. I'm counting on you."

Millie hung up, feeling a little smug but a lot annoyed.

She had been the top employee at Rumley & Riggs for the past several years. The idea that he would fire her over one account made her more than annoyed, actually; it made her angry, but she had his permission to stay at the old hotel. That was good enough for now.

Lonny came out and sat beside her. "So, was it good news?"

"For you, great news. Maybe." She studied his face. "You look beat, though. You could probably use a night in your own place."

He raised his eyebrows. "What's the good news?"

Millie didn't want him to think she didn't care, that it was only about the hotel. He needed to be near his dad, not hanging out at a hotel and waiting for ghosts. They could do that on another night.

"Millie," he took her hand, "is the good news not good news?"

She winced. "Mr. Rumley has offered to pay you double what you made before, per night, if you'll stay at the hotel and guard it against vandals until the twenty-seventh."

Lonny laughed. "You had me there. I was worried something terrible was going on. That you were packing up and leaving or something." He wiped both hands over his face. "So, you're telling me that your boss is willing to pay me, basically, a month's salary to watch what should rightfully be my own property, for five nights?" He grinned with disbelief and chuckled.

"You haven't come forward and claimed it yet, but yeah." She lifted a shoulder. "I'm just worried about your parents, and you. You look tired."

"Mills, I can sleep almost anywhere. Sleeping in a bed tonight—" He appeared sheepish.

"You slept in the truck, didn't you?" Millie shook her head, trying to suppress a grin.

"I told you I wouldn't leave you at the hotel alone. I

meant it."

She should have known. Lonny had never let her down, not in all the years she'd known him. Always true to his word. She had grown cynical, in part because of Mama's bitterness, but also because of her own perceived disappointments. She had fully expected Lonny to find her when she was eighteen, to ride in on his white horse and take her away. Come to find out, he had tried. Fate had just insisted they wait a little longer before reconnecting.

"What are you thinking?" Lonny brought her away from her thoughts.

"I'm thinking that I wanted you to know . . ." Millie had a hard time putting her emotions into words. "I want you to know that it wouldn't matter to me if you dug ditches for a living." She looked away, blinking and trying to keep her emotions reigned in. Lonny touched her arm and she turned to him. "You don't need money for me to care about you. I hope you know that."

"I do." Lonny pulled her into his embrace.

"You know what else I'm thinking?" She pulled away and grinned.

"What?"

"I'm thinking that we need to go out for a nice steak dinner. My treat. Or rather, Rumley and Riggs' treat. I haven't had anything to eat and I'm starving."

"We'll beat the dinner crowd." He led her toward the truck.

"Yeah." She smirked, then saw he was serious. "You have a dinner crowd in the middle of the week?" This area had changed a lot in fourteen years.

He opened the truck door for her, then hurried to the driver's side and jumped in. "There could be a dinner crowd." He took her hands in his and then pulled them up for examination. "What happened to your long Godiva nails?" His forehead wrinkled.

"They're not Godiva nails, and I'm trying something different."

"I like it," he said. "Let's get out of here. I'm famished, yeah."

They went to an isolated restaurant on the top of a mesa. It had windows overlooking the valley, and the city lights below made the place feel magical. Millie tried to find the Ballard hotel, but it was too far away. The dinner crowd hadn't yet shown up, and it felt as if they'd bought out the restaurant in order to dine alone.

"I was thinking." She stirred her mashed potatoes. "We don't know how much GK Investments has been paying on the property tax lien. Sometimes big corporations negotiate prices. Now that we know for certain that your family is the rightful heirs, and we can prove it, we need to find out how much it will take to pay off Mr. Kappel." The man was a creep. She would be glad to be rid of him as a client.

Lonny cut his steak and took a bite. "That's a good idea. We can go back to the courthouse tomorrow and ask."

"I'm glad you're finally open to the idea of being an heir."

"As you said, there's no disputing it. But actually, I've been having these feelings about the Ballard property for a while."

"Why didn't you say anything?"

"It made me angry and ashamed that I couldn't afford it and would never be able to. Now that I know the property should be my inheritance, I'd like to know by how much I missed owning my own hotel. It'll make Pop happy."

"I've got money in savings. I could loan it to you."

"I'm not taking your money, Millie."

Millie, huh. "I wouldn't be giving it to you. It would be a business loan. We'll have papers drawn up at the bank." She plastered a smile on her face, feeling a bit awkward.

"I don't know."

"You don't have to decide tonight. We don't even know how much it is. I may not even be able to help." Millie changed the subject after that. She wouldn't press the issue. But neither one of them was talkative through the rest of the meal.

Lonny rubbed his forehead. "I'm getting this weird vibe, like we need to head to the hotel and spend the evening there."

Millie called for the check. "Are you sure?" She hadn't sensed anything.

"Yeah. Just all of a sudden, I got this feeling that something's not right." After the bill was paid, Lonny pulled her chair out for her and then led the way outside. "It's kind of like you said the other day, it's like ants crawling all over me." They got into Lonny's truck and headed toward Solomon.

Twenty-Three

It was dusk when they arrived at the hotel. A construction truck and a black Jaguar were parked out front.

"What the—" Lonny slammed the truck into park and leapt from his vehicle. "Stay here." He raced inside.

Millie wasn't about to wait in the truck. She got out and followed him. When some people had a little bit of money, it made them feel entitled, which was apparently Gerald Kappel's issue. What right did he have? She marched to the front door and stopped.

Her heart sank and she let out an anguished cry. Clearly Kappel hadn't found what he wanted in the cellar. The furniture was piled in the corner like garbage. Kenny Evans, apparently unfazed by Millie disabling his backhoe, wore a dust mask and wielded a large sledgehammer. He had destroyed half of the lobby counter, and splintered wood was scattered all around. Millie strode to him. "I can't believe you're involved in this vandalism." She yanked the sledgehammer from his grasp. The weight of it sent it to the floor. Millie jumped out of its way and then turned to the noise behind her.

Lonny and Kappel were arguing in the middle of the room. Millie stormed over to them, shoving Kappel's shoulder. "What are you doing?" Millie demanded. "This isn't your property yet. You gave me the key. That's breaking and entering. How did you get in here?"

Before he could answer, Lonny cut in. "Millie, drive my truck out to the highway and call 9-1-1." Lonny turned back to Kappel. "We'll get the sheriff over here and he'll decide what rights you have."

Millie ran out the door, drove the truck to the highway, and called. "There's been a break-in and extensive vandalism at the old Ballard Hotel. The person responsible is still there and refuses to leave." They promised an officer would be right over.

Millie's heart thudded. Gerald Kappel held a lot of power. He could destroy her, her career, and everything she had worked for within a day. He might also destroy Rumley & Riggs in the process. She took several calming breaths. What mattered was that she would do the right thing and not let herself be intimidated.

Twenty minutes later, dust flew everywhere as Sheriff Adams and two deputies drove in with their sirens blaring. By that time, Lonny and Kappel had backed off and were waiting tensely. The investor strongly believed he had every right to be there and to start demolition ahead of schedule. Millie fumed at his feelings of entitlement as she surveyed the destruction of the front desk area. They were lucky Lonny had been impressed to be there. Otherwise, Kappel would have destroyed the whole place.

"What seems to be the problem?" Sheriff Adams asked. Two deputies that Millie didn't recognize flanked his sides.

Kappel raised his shoulders and cleared his throat. "I've been paying the tax lien on this property for ten years, and the sale is due to go through this Tuesday. The place has stood vacant for over a hundred years." He flailed his arms out. "I don't see what harm it'll cause if I start my renovations a few days early. My wife is insisting that we go to New Hampshire for the holidays to spend time with her parents, and we won't be back for the better part of a month. I'm a busy man and I need this project to go through on schedule."

The man was a good liar. "When we talked the other morning, I told you to stay away from the property until the sale becomes final." Millie put her hands on her hips. "There's still a chance an heir will make claim on the property. If so, I want it in writing that you will restore the lobby to its original charm."

Kappel snorted. "The place is a dump. That won't take much." He looked at the sheriff and deputies. "Okay, sure. If some loser comes in at the last second, with the money to make good, and wants to take possession, I will restore the lobby."

"Have you done damage elsewhere?" Sheriff Adams pulled out a pad and pen.

"I've been in the cellar, the attic, and the suite." He nodded toward the double doors. "Ms. Crump has been there, too."

Ignoring his implication, Sheriff Adams turned to Kenny. "What's your involvement in this?"

"I gave him the key to get in, but I didn't know." Kenny shrugged. "I thought he was on the up and up."

Millie hardly believed that. He had wielded the sledgehammer. "Did Mr. Kappel offer you part of the treasure if you helped find it?"

The color drained from Kenny's face. "Still. I thought he was legit."

"With this kind of damage," Sheriff Adams said, "it does appear that you were looking for something." He lifted his eyebrows. "You're really committing felony vandalism based on local folklore?" He scoffed.

"It's nobody's business what I was doing. I'll just start it up again when I get back." Gerald Kappel glared at the sheriff and then turned to Millie. "I'm leaving now. Going away for the holiday, but I'll be back and you'll be sorry you interfered."

The sheriff stood forward. "Is that a threat?"

"Ms. Crump knows full well that it's a promise." He turned and started to leave the hotel.

"I'm sorry, Mr. Kappel but you're coming with me. You, too, Kenny. This is breaking and entering coupled with felony vandalism." Sheriff Adams nodded to his deputies. "Cuff them and take them to the station."

"I'll just have my lawyer get me out," Gerald Kappel said, then turned to the deputy cuffing him. "Watch yourself. My watch costs more than you make in a year."

Kenny resisted the cuffs, talking to the sheriff, "Now, John, I was hired by Mr. Kappel—how was I supposed to know he didn't have the legal right to enter? And you know I'm not a flight risk; I can't go to jail."

"That's fine, Kenny. You're released on your own recognizance, but you'll still have your day in court and I'll expect you to be there."

He nodded once. "Thank you, sheriff." He took a few steps toward the door, and glared at Millie and Lonny as he left.

The deputies started outside with Mr. Kappel, but he stopped in the doorway. "What about my Jaguar?"

Sheriff Adams tapped his fingers together. "One of my deputies can drive it to the station if you'd like or else I can have it impounded."

After a moment's hesitation, Kappel took the keys from his pocket and handed them to a deputy. "There had better not be a scratch on it when this mess is resolved."

The deputies left, and the sheriff turned to Lonny. "Well, I suggest you all leave now. I guess we'll have to set guards out." He shook his head and sighed.

Millie stepped forward. "I'm Millie Crump. My boss, Mr. Rumley of Rumley & Riggs, is in charge of the sale, and he has agreed to pay Gila Valley Property Managers—Mr. Medina," she indicated Lonny—"to guard the place each night until the sale becomes final. Mr. Kappel can take over at that time."

After another half-hour, the sheriff was satisfied that the hotel would be safe for the evening. He said goodbye and went to his vehicle. Lonny and Millie faced the door until the sheriff left.

Millie turned to Lonny. "Anna's never going to speak to me again. And it's doubtful that I'll have a job at Rumley and Riggs after tonight."

"It'll all work out." Lonny pulled her toward him and kissed her forehead.

"I suppose," Millie said. "In the meantime, I think we should sleep down here to see if Emerson comes."

Lonny rubbed his chin, nodding. "There aren't wood shards in the parlor and we'll be able to watch each step of Emerson's actions."

"There might be a built-in safe behind the divan in the parlor. I saw him go back here." They went upstairs and got their bedding, set it up in the parlor, and lay there waiting and watching. "Do you think Kappel scared him off?" Millie winced. The man scared her.

"Nah. He'll show up. We still have stuff to learn."

Twenty-Four

Lonny rested inside his makeshift bedroll watching Millie sleep. Morning rays filtered through the sheer curtains at the front window and encased her in a heavenly glow. She was beautiful and at peace.

She yawned and peeked her eyes open. "Emerson didn't shown up."

He reached out and guided a stray hair from her face. "No."

She sat up, pushing her hair back. "What if the damage Mr. Kappel did is keeping Emerson from reenacting his death? I wanted you to see the whole reenactment and get your opinion. What if Emerson never returns? If so, what would that mean—that he moved to his eternal reward—or is he still stuck somewhere in-between?"

Sometimes her questions were exhausting, but Lonny just smiled in return.

She crept out of her bedroll and walked to the front desk, tip-toeing around wood shards with a hand to her heart. "Seeing this damage makes me physically ill. Thanks to your intuition, we were able to save the hotel. If we hadn't gotten here in time, Kappel might have destroyed the whole place." She picked up the larger wood pieces and leaned them against the wall, then went to the closet and came back with a broom to sweep up the debris.

Lonny got up and joined her. "Maybe we can put this back together." He scratched his head. "I've got some framing material in my truck. Enough to set this up."

Millie looked at the mess, seeming unsure. But he had handyman skills she wasn't aware of. He picked up a large chunk of wood and examined it. "We could make a frame and attach these big pieces to it."

"Yeah. That might work. I don't know if it'll bring Emerson back tonight, but we've got to at least try."

Lonny went outside and got the tools from the back of his truck, and they spent the morning recreating the front desk to the best of their ability. Millie didn't do a lot, but luckily she knew the difference between a nail and a hammer, and was able to get things from his truck and to hold on to boards while he sawed them.

Millie stood back, her eyebrows lifted. "It's kind of pitiful, really."

"The frame is good, yeah." The middle showed large gaps between each piece. The in-between pieces had shattered under the weight of the sledgehammer. "Kenny did a great job of destroying the original mahogany."

"Hopefully all that matters is that the end of the counter, near where Emerson was shot, is put together." Millie touched it almost reverently, then gathered her things. "I'm going upstairs to get cleaned up before we go to the county office. I bet they close early today." She ran upstairs.

Lonny gathered his tools and put them in the back of his truck, then went inside and put the furniture back in place. Millie came down the stairs.

"Done already?" He thought she'd be longer. Then he saw her—her hair swept to the side like she'd worn it as a teen. The heavy makeup had been replaced with a thin layer of foundation and mascara. He couldn't take his eyes off her. The corner of his lip turned up with his approval.

"What?" She stopped. "Do I look ridiculous? Should I go up and try again?"

"It's just … you look …" Lonny felt his face heat, and that embarrassed him.

"I'll take that as a compliment." She gave him a flirty smile.

"Yeah, well, it's my turn." He grabbed his things and hurried upstairs. The water was cold and the flow constricted—one more expense that would keep his family from taking ownership. After a quick shower, he applied his favorite cologne. It had driven Millie crazy before. Hopefully, it still did.

When Lonny came down, Millie grinned. "You clean up nice." She sniffed the air, prowling around him. "My favorite cologne." She lifted on her toes and kissed his cheek.

That was the reaction he'd hoped for. "You like it?"

"That's the cologne you used to wear." Millie sighed, then crooked her arm in his. "Let's go find out how much the tax lien is."

A half hour later, they sat in the county recorder's office, looking at the paper that showed the total amount owed to repay the Ballard property taxes. Millie looked at Lonny. "There must be a mix-up," she whispered.

There were certainly fewer zeros than he expected. He tamped down a smile. "You're sure this is correct?" he asked Alex, the clerk.

"Yes." Alex pointed out the information. "About ten years ago, someone protested the taxes. The property began being taxed solely as farmland, which is exponentially lower than commercial property. There's a note here saying that the hotel isn't inhabitable."

"Yeah, it isn't," Lonny agreed. "It'd take tens of thousands to bring it up to code so it could be a hotel again," He looked at the amount due and the heavy weight of doubt lifted. He'd had feelings about the hotel, but until now he'd pushed them away, believing it was beyond his reach, financially. "I could sell two of my best steers and put together that much, and then use the property for range."

"Isn't that what GK Investments was planning to do?" Millie said in an frustrated tone. "I think Emerson's whole point is having someone to love the hotel like he and Samantha loved it, not just the property." She worked her jaw.

"I won't tear it down, but I don't have the money to fix it up. You know that." Pop's cancer treatments hadn't been free. Lonny looked at the clerk, finding it hard to tamp down his smile. "I'd like to make an official claim on this property. Where do I go to do that?"

"The third floor. Turn right at the elevator."

They went up the elevator and Lonny made his claim, but Millie didn't feel right about it—not because she didn't want him to take ownership—of course she did—it was the disappointment of not being able to care for the hotel. Although she had only recently been inside, the hotel held a lot of memories for her, and it had been Emerson's home. It still was his home in a ghostly sense. It was a unique part of her and Lonny's history, and also had a unique history of its own that made it special.

They could fix it up, put it on the historical register and turn it into a bed and breakfast as well as use the dining area for a restaurant. Property could be purchased anywhere; the Ballard Hotel had potential. If the Medinas had the money. She said a silent prayer for her Christmas miracle.

Lonny drove them to a fast-food place and they enjoyed a quick bite of lunch. He was a good man and Millie enjoyed every minute of their meal. As they left the restaurant, he said, "I need to go and check on my folks and take care of the animals, and then I need to get caught up on work. You wanna come?"

Millie had a better idea. "Not this time. Meet me at the hotel tonight?" She needed to go to the store.

Lonny gave her a sour expression. "Are you sure you want me there?"

Not if he was going to be all surly. "Absolutely. That is, unless you've changed your mind." He wasn't going to put this, whatever it was, on her.

"I haven't changed my mind, I was just wondering if you had." He opened his truck door and she scooted in. They drove to the old hotel in relative silence. Millie had been a wreck when Mama got sick. So, even though she wasn't ready to forget his weird attitude just yet, she did understand he was under a lot of stress.

Tomorrow was Christmas Eve, and although they had discovered a lot, and she was able to tell Kappel to stand down in regards to destroying the Ballard property, Millie didn't feel as though her Christmas miracle had been granted. Not really.

The first place Millie went after leaving the county building was to Main Street in Safford. She was tired of being cold. Plus, she wanted to wear something Lonny would like. Tomorrow was special, after all. She found an open boutique that sold women's clothing and parked. There was nothing to her current standard of taste, but she found a soft, Christmassy sweater-blouse. She purchased that and a nicely fitting pair of jeans as well as a pair of comfortable shoes. On her way out, she dropped her designer heels in the trash. They were ruined from walking on uneven surfaces.

Next, she went to the grocery store to buy ingredients for tamales. Mrs. Medina had taught her to make them the way Lonny liked them best, and Millie would invite the Medinas and Lonny over for a nice Christmas Eve dinner. Tamales were an all day process.

She picked out fresh produce for a side and a salad, picked out a nice pork roast, and headed toward the aisle where she hoped to find the masa. Then she spotted Len Begay walking toward her in uniform, and pushing an empty cart.

"Merry almost-Christmas." He stopped beside her. "I hear that Lonny Medina has good news."

She crossed her arms. "What are you talking about?" Regardless of the fact that he held a responsible position in the community, Millie didn't believe he'd changed that much in his personal life.

"The old abandoned hotel and all that property is his now. Didn't you know?"

"Oh. Yes." She nodded. "But he barely stated his claim an hour ago. How did you find out so soon?" And why did he care?

Len ignored her question. "Does he have plans for it? I mean, you both love the place—or you seem to. I can't imagine him tearing anything down, and it's too shabby to live in. Right?"

Millie told him about Lonny's plan to raise cattle on the land.

He smiled. "Perfect. So, he'll he keep the buildings then, or does he plan to demolish everything like the other buyers?"

Len's interest seemed off, as if he was a little too interested. "He indicated that he won't tear anything down."

"He doesn't seem to mind staying in the dump, though—I mean, he's been staying there now. Right? He'll probably want to move in—Nah, he has his own house—

but he'll wanna move the cattle over right away. But he probably doesn't have hay for the barn. Does he?" He shook his head. "Hay's hard to move. I'm sure he'll want to wait until he uses what he's got stored at his parents' house." He nodded to himself.

When had Len Begay ever cared what the Medinas were doing? She answered anyway. It wasn't a secret. "Even though we've been staying there, as you're aware, the hotel needs new plumbing and that includes hot water. The electrical needs updating too. It isn't currently livable."

"Right." He nodded. "Now that he's going to be a wealthy man, you're probably going to quit seeing me and go off and marry Lonny." He gave her a frown.

"Owning that property doesn't make him wealthy." What were all these questions about?

"Will you join me for lunch?"

"Lonny and I already had lunch." She hated just blowing him off, but also wondered if the deputy was the cause of the rumors regarding the two of them.

Len frowned, then immediately smiled. "Oh, come on. Now that your job is done, you'll probably be going home soon. When will I ever see you again?"

"You probably won't. I have all of these groceries and I need to get them back to the hotel." She didn't want to tell him she was making tamales for fear he'd think he was invited over.

"That's not a problem. I'll talk the manager into letting you store everything in the walk-in cooler until you get back. I need to go to my house to care for my animals and I hoped you would join me." He lifted his eyebrows, his hand resting on her cart.

Millie shook her head. "It's been really nice getting to know you again and I really appreciate how nice you've been—it's helped me to feel welcomed—but Lonny's dad has cancer. He's not doing well and I plan to spend my remaining time in the Gila Valley with the Medinas."

He tapped his cheek, smiling. "How about a kiss goodbye?"

"I'm sorry, Len, but it just can't work out between us when my heart is with someone else." She patted his hand that rested on the cart, and then pushed it gently out of his grasp. "I do feel honored that you considered me." She pushed the cart away, pleased with herself for being kind, yet firm. She didn't need to spend another questionable second with a man who only made her wish for someone else.

Twenty-Five

Lonny met her at the hotel at dusk. Millie looked up from a book she had found in the attic. "I think I'm going to write a book about Emerson's history when he was alive, our experiences with him as a ghost, starting when we were children, and include your discover that your family are his descendants. And I bet we could find some investors to help with remodeling the hotel. And . . ." she trailed off at Lonny's expression. "Is everything okay?"

"That all sounds nice; we can talk about it later. I wanted to ask you something." He averted his eyes.

Millie's first thought was he'd decided to let her loan him the money—she didn't have enough to remodel the hotel, though. She put the book down and went to him. "I can help. I'm happy to help, but I don't have that much in savings."

Lonny's eyebrows pulled together. He shook his head. "No, it's not about the hotel. I wondered . . ." he looked away again. "We used to love going to *Las Posadas* at Christmastime. They're gathering for it right now. Will you go with me?"

Millie inhaled, deeply. Las Posadas was a Christmas celebration that portrayed Joseph and Mary's journey as they looked for shelter that holy night. Millie rubbed her hand across her mouth, considering. It had been years since she had attended one, and this would be the second to last evening of the nine-day event. However, she was asking for a Christmas miracle, and what better way to show God she was earnest? "Yes, let's go. I don't have anything to wear to it, though." As a young girl, she had worn an angel costume.

"That doesn't matter. Only the children dress up. I brought you a coat, but we need to hurry." He took her hand. They locked up and hurried to the little church where a group of people were gathered. At first she hesitated, feeling unsure, but others greeted them and helped her feel welcomed. They were given a lit candle and a board with handmade clay figurines representing Mary on a donkey and Joseph standing beside her. She remembered helping to make similar clay figurines as a teen.

As they walked down the street, they sang holy Christmas carols, and Millie's memory of walking the streets as a child, her heart filled with love and faith, filled her once again. When they reached the first home of Las Posadas, which was decorated with paper lanterns and a pine bough, the children in the group stepped closer to the door and sang the song of Las Posadas:

"In the name of heaven, I ask you for shelter, for my beloved wife can go no farther."

The people inside the home sang their response: *"This is not an inn, Get on with you, I cannot open the door, you might be a rogue."*

Millie's heart warmed at the sight of the little angels, and the boys dressed in old robes. When it was time, the group walked to the next home while singing more carols. She walked along the street, feeling as though each step was on holy ground. The second home also had a pine bough on the door and a paper lantern at the doorstep. The children came forward, repeating the song of Las Posadas, the lilting melody reaching to the sky. Once again they were turned away. Millie linked arms with Lonny and leaned in, giving him a hug. "Thank you for bringing me. It's just what I needed."

"Me too." Lonny bent down and kissed her forehead. They continued on, the children singing at the chosen homes until they got to the fourth home. The children sang to the people inside, and when the family recognized Mary and Josef, and allowed them to enter, everyone joined in singing the final verse of Las Posadas: *"Enter holy pilgrims, pilgrims receive this corner, not this poor dwelling but my heart. Tonight is for joy, for pleasure and rejoicing, for tonight we will give lodging to the Mother of God the Son."*

As Millie sang the words, her heart filled with light and love. She knew that God loved her. She finally realized that she loved him, too, and tears filled her eyes as they walked into the final home to receive a Christmas feast. A colorful star piñata was in the backyard and all of the children rushed outside.

Lonny bent down, touching his head to hers, and wiped the tears from her eyes. "Merry Christmas, Millie Crump."

In answer, she reached up and kissed his cheek.

They didn't stay long at the feast, but went back to the old hotel in the hope that Emerson would come. Maybe the commotion of the previous night had scared him away or rather disrupted his ritual.

"Ya know, I believe that this will be the night that we can see Emerson's complete routine from beginning to end. It might help us figure out where he put his winnings." Millie gave him a bright smile, hoping to encourage him and her both.

Lonny frowned. "I thought you didn't believe in the treasure."

"The money was here at one time; who's to say it isn't still here somewhere?" She tilted her head and shrugged. The odds were against it, but it was worth this small effort on their part.

"You always did like a sleep over." He shook his head and smirked, then he ran up the stairs ahead of her.

"Hey!" She took off after him. "It's not only about the sleepover. We could have missed a vital clue. It's possible." She pulled the bedding off the bed she had made that morning. Then, so he wouldn't think she was keeping secrets, she said, "I saw Len Begay at the grocery store today."

"Yeah?" Lonny followed her down the stairs, carrying his bedding.

"He already knew about your claim on the hotel and was asking a bunch of questions about whether or not you plan to live here. How would he have known so soon, and why does he care?" She folded and rolled her bedding into a bedroll like she had previously.

"You think he's trying to find the treasure?"

"That would make sense." Millie nodded. "I wonder if he's been helping Kappel search for it or if he's working on his own."

"You said Kappel has been down in the cellar. Let's go check it out." Lonny stepped over his bedroll. They grabbed Millie's flashlight and went around to the back of the hotel. Millie was relieved to see that Kenny Evans had removed the backhoe. "They can't do too much damage by hand, I'm sure."

Lonny lifted the hatch and Millie went in, shining the flashlight in front of her. There were more holes and someone had started shoveling dirt from the walls. Lonny stepped beside her. "It looks as though someone has been busy."

Millie grimaced. "There are definitely more holes now than when I looked the other day. What should we do?" She knew Emerson left the lobby and went somewhere. Just because she didn't think the treasure was down here didn't mean it wasn't. It didn't seem like anyone had discovered any treasure, though, or they wouldn't still be looking.

"I think the lumber yard is still open. Let's go get some supplies. I'll make a new door and buy a padlock for it. That ought to keep them out."

"A new door will probably work. I bought a chain and a lock, but someone used the backhoe and ripped it off." She walked to the corner of the cellar and picked up a handful of quart jars. "Help me get these back into the kitchen. I don't want them to get broken. You can use them and that antique pressure canner to decorate; maybe not the dining room, but at least you can put them in the kitchen." She nodded toward the canner.

"Decorate?" Lonny shook his head. "You're not going to give up on restoring the hotel, are you."

"I hope not." She gave him a big smile and carried the jars up the steps. Lonny followed her into the hotel's kitchen with another load. "And look what I found the other day." She showed him the cute tin with recipes. "You could put a petting zoo with farm animals out in the barn. It's the perfect set up for a bed and breakfast. Fresh eggs. Fresh milk. Homemade cheese. Homemade ice cream." She sighed. "It will be perfect."

Lonny strode forward, took her into his arms, and took her breath away with a kiss. When he released her, she was weak in the knees. She worked up her best western accent and said, "I do declare, Lonny Medina, what has gotten into you?" She held onto him for support and gazed into his eyes, her heart still pounding.

He smiled warmly. "You were always a dreamer.

I'm glad that hasn't changed." He grabbed her hand and headed to his truck.

They arrived at the lumberyard just minutes before closing time and hurried through the store to get what they needed. Then, back at the hotel, they worked in the moonlight and with the truck's headlights to build the hatch.

Millie placed her hands on her hips and looked at their handiwork. "After breaking apart the front desk, I think Kappel is fairly satisfied that the treasure isn't in the lobby. I'm not certain he believes it's down here anymore, either, but I'm glad we're not taking any chances. The attic still has unopened boxes. You want to look up there next?" Knowing that the Medinas were the heirs to the hotel and that they couldn't afford the necessary repairs to make the hotel livable made her desperate for a treasure.

"Not right now. I need to go help my folks." He picked up his tools and put them back into his tool bag.

"Absolutely. I bet they're hungry. If you don't mind, I can pay for our meals." The Medinas had done their share of providing food.

"That's kind, but it's late. They've already had dinner from leftovers in the fridge. You can stay and search through the attic if you'd like, but I need to check on my folks and feed the livestock."

Millie grimaced. "Uh, no. I don't want to stay here by myself."

"Still afraid of ghosts?" Lonny smirked.

"Not at all." She huffed. "I'm more afraid of the living." Gerald Kappel was a powerful man and she didn't know what he was capable of or how far he'd take his desire for treasure. "Plus, I haven't seen your parents yet today, and I really would like to go and help. I'll take my own car, though. That way, you can go out and feed your animals, and I can go inside and visit with your folks."

Lonny's eyebrows dipped as he frowned, but he didn't argue with her. They locked up the hotel and she followed him to the Medina's. When they got there, Mami greeted them in a panic. "Your father, he has fallen! Come and help!"

Millie's heart jolted. This couldn't be happening. She followed on Lonny's heels as he raced inside and found his father sitting and leaning against the wall. "Pop! Are you okay?" He knelt beside him. "Do you think you broke any bones?

"No. I was dizzy and then the floor hit me in the face." He reached out for help. "My old bones won't let me stand. *Hija*, come help an old man who's too foolish to stay on his feet."

"You're not foolish." Millie rushed to his other side and she and Lonny helped him to stand.

"Pop. We're going to take you to the hospital just to make sure there's nothing wrong." Lonny held him around the waist.

"I don't need a hospital," he replied, but allowed them to help him out the door.

Mami rushed around, grabbing her purse and hurrying beside her husband.

"I'll follow you there." Millie ran to her car, grateful she had thought to drive separately.

The nursing staff took Mr. Medina right into a partitioned space in the ER. Millie, Lonny and Mrs. Medina waited while he was taken to X-ray to make sure he hadn't broken any bones. Hours later, it was determined that he had no broken bones, but was dehydrated. They hooked him to an IV and wheeled him to a room. "He'll need to stay overnight," the nurse said.

Mrs. Medina sat beside him and stroked his hair. "Will he be okay?"

"There's nothing to worry about. If everything goes

well, he'll be released in the morning. It'll take that long to get adequate fluids back in him."

Millie went to the bed and stood opposite of Mami. Papi reached for her hand, and she held it. Tears streamed down her face and she wiped them away, embarrassed to cry in front of him, but the situation was too similar to Mama's four years ago. "You be well, *Papi*. I'm making tamales tomorrow for Christmas Eve. You'll want some, won't you?"

"It isn't Christmas Eve without a good tamale. I will be well for tamales." He patted her hand. "Now don't you cry; I need you to take good care of my beautiful Rosa."

"I will, *Papi*. I will." Millie leaned forward and kissed his forehead. "You be sure to get a good rest, and listen to the nurses."

Mr. Medina nodded and closed his eyes.

Millie followed Lonny to the Medinas' home and helped Mami get settled. The sweet woman wanted to go straight to bed. "The sooner I go to sleep, the sooner morning will come."

Millie kissed her cheek. "Good night, Mami." She wasn't sure what to do. She itched to be at the hotel and to watch Emerson's routine, but it wasn't good to leave Mami alone. "Why don't we stay here in case your mom needs anything? It's not right for her to be by herself. And perhaps the hospital will call."

Lonny walked forward, facing her, and kissed her forehead. "Thank you."

"It is my pleasure. Always." Millie put her arms around Lonny and held onto him. "Papi will be okay. He has to be." She didn't know what she would do if he didn't come home.

Twenty-Six

Lonny wasn't sure how he was going to tell Millie his news and discuss with her the last rumors he'd heard. She'd gotten angry the first time he'd shared gossip, and he was simply too exhausted to deal with more problems. He wanted to go home. To his home. He wanted Pop to be well. None of that was going to happen.

He walked into the hotel ready to tell her, and took a whiff of the air. He smacked his forehead with the heel of his hand. She was making tamales for them and he had forgotten. His mouth watered with the scent of rich spices, roasted chili peppers and cumin. This kind gesture made him love her all the more. He knew she had spent the day making them—there was no way to get around that. He also knew she was doing it for him and his parents. And he would ruin their special Christmas Eve with this news. He bit back his disappointment.

The dining area was set with a tablecloth and china for four. Millie was in the kitchen humming a Christmas tune. "I'm sorry, Mama, but this is for me," she muttered.

This was going to be harder than he thought.

She noticed him standing in the doorway. "I figured

we could eat here," she said brightly. "Did you bring your parents—was *Papi* well enough to come?" She glanced toward the door. "I just thought it would be fun to have your first meal as owners of the hotel, here. Plus, there's no mess for them to worry about."

He clutched his hands in front of him, hoping she would know he only wanted the best for her. He would tell her the easy news first. "Pop had a hard day today and Mom refused to come without him."

"Oh. Okay." Millie chewed her lip for a moment as she took in the news. "We can go there. It's not a problem. Just give me time to pack everything up."

"There's more," he said. "A steer is stuck in the barbed wire fence. I need to take care of it." He hesitated, not wanting to say more.

"Oh." Her shoulders slumped. "Dinner'll wait. I mean, I wouldn't want the animal to suffer or possibly die."

The woman was a vision of loveliness. She had on a soft-looking red sweater—and jeans. Those were new. He gulped, staring at her as he took in her beauty and prayed she would understand his heart.

Her brows furrowed. "You'll come back, right, and we can have dinner together then, or maybe go to Las Posadas?"

He winced. "There's something else and I'm not sure it should wait. After that, I'm not certain you'll want me to come back."

She faltered and stepped back. "What? What's more important than an injured steer?"

"Maybe we should sit down." He moved to a nearby table, extending a chair for her and then sitting opposite of her. "You'll be honest with me, yeah?"

"Of course I'll be honest with you." Something was

horribly wrong. Millie gulped, nerves etching up her spine. "Do you need help with the steer?" she asked, trying to ease the tension in the room.

"Millie." He reached for her hand. He was shaking! "How do you really feel about Deputy Begay?—I know it doesn't matter what I think about him in that regard, but I'm not certain he's changed as much as you think he has."

Why was he asking this? "I told you before that we are just friends. Not even that, really. At first I thought he was a charmer, but there's something suspicious about him. He popped up yesterday while I was at the grocery store asking all kinds of questions about you and the property. He already knew that you'd put in your claim as the heir, and it was less than an hour later."

"So, you aren't in a relationship with him?" He gazed into her eyes, but she had nothing to hide in that regard.

"Absolutely not. Why?"

"You're a beautiful woman and any man would be lucky to have you, but I have to wonder if some of it has been staged by him. I just don't understand why." He glanced at her worriedly.

"Well, he came to the hotel the other night with pie and ice cream, but he wasn't inappropriate. I mean, I started to get nervous for a moment, but Emerson chased him away." She smiled at that memory. "And like I said, he showed up at the grocery store, then after asking all those questions, he wanted to take me to lunch. I said, no. He tried persuading me, and even tried to get me to kiss his cheek. I told him goodbye and that I'd probably never see him again. What was gossip-worthy about that?"

"I'm not sure. People see the two of you together and apparently they feel it's their duty to talk to me about it." Lonny wiped his hand over his face.

He looked stressed and tired. Millie couldn't be mad at him. Not on Christmas Eve. Not knowing everything he was going through. But their special evening had been spoiled; it made her heart hurt.

"Look," she said quietly, "I don't know if he has an ulterior motive, or even what it would be." She let go of his hand and stood. "I'll get you some tamales to go. If you'd like to stay the night here, you're welcome to come back when you're finished. If you need to stay with your parents tonight or if it takes all night with the steer, I'll understand." Millie turned toward the kitchen and wiped at a tear. She'd had such high hopes for a special Christmas Eve—her first as a believing adult.

She heard him walking behind her. "I'm sorry." He rubbed her shoulders. "I just felt you deserved to know. I'm sorry," he repeated.

Millie couldn't look at him. She got the aluminum foil and wrapped several tamales for him. Then she wrapped four more. "These are for your parents."

She could feel his gaze, but she wasn't ready to see him and guided him toward the door. "You'd better get out of here before it's too late to save your steer."

"Yeah." He nodded and left.

The lobby closed in around her as she stood looking at the door Lonny had gone through, listening to the truck engine roar to life, and the sound of tires on hard dirt—and remembering the night her father had left. This was different, of course, but she felt abandoned just the same. It was evening, and Emerson started his nightly routine after sunset, unless Kappel returned. She had no doubt he knew an heir had been found and was angry about it. Millie didn't want to be there alone.

Why hadn't Lonny asked for her help? She would have helped—would have done anything to keep from being alone on Christmas Eve. But what did she know about rescuing cattle? And she knew nothing about barbed wire, not really. Okay, question answered, but she still hated being alone on Christmas Eve and she could have had dinner with Mami and Papi.

In the kitchen, Millie laid out the remaining steamed tamales on the counter to cool and placed two on a plate for her. Then, she went into the dining room and sat at the table she had previously set with a white linen tablecloth and the Ballard china and ate her special Christmas meal alone. The tamales tasted good, if she said so herself. And she did. After dinner, she washed her plate and the other dishes, and then scrubbed the counters until the kitchen sparkled. She turned off the light and went into the foyer.

Emerson was there having an argument. "It's too late now. What's done is done. It's not gambling when I know I'll win. After tonight, I'll be able to pay off all our debts and shut down the whole operation."

This scene was new to her. Only Emerson could see whom he was arguing with, and she knew better than to interrupt him. He was more like a hologram as he went through his nightly ritual. She knew any noise or activity would disturb him and he'd disappear. Millie held still and watched. Maybe seeing more of that fateful day really would give her new clues to help Lonny's family.

After the ghostly argument, Emerson turned toward the dining hall and disappeared. Millie realized at that point, he probably went out to the cockfights in the barn because he didn't have the treasure yet. According to the historical society, someone must have gone out later and told him Samantha was in labor, and somehow he came in wearing Bronco Bill's hat. That was after he had won. She hoped that he had won more than that ragged old hat in the attic. It could be worth good money to a collector, but doubtful it would be enough to restore the hotel.

Spending Christmas Eve alone with a ghost was about as lonely as she had ever felt. She would have had a better time in Phoenix. Millie couldn't get mad, though; a steer stuck in barbed wire was a big deal. It was probably tricky getting it loose. And poor Lonny having everyone he knew telling him every time they saw her with Deputy Begay. That was just wrong. Millie shook her head, but at the thought of the deputy, chills went up her spine. He was up to something. She wouldn't stay by herself in the parlor all night, so she hurried toward the stairs to sleep in a proper bed. She had only taken a few steps when she heard Emerson.

"Samantha, darlin', come and see what I won." Emerson came through the back door wearing Bronco Bill's hat and seeming to hold something heavy.

He didn't behave as though he knew his wife was in labor. Millie watched from the stairs. Emerson went through the motions of placing his invisible load on the front desk. He rushed to the grandfather clock in the parlor, took something out, and then hurried to the drawers of the front desk, disappearing behind it for a moment, then stood and pushed against the wall. It seemed that he put his load inside the wall. Millie watched, fascinated. Afterward, he went back to the clock.

He perked up, turning his head. "Samantha, Darlin', what's wrong?" He strode purposefully toward their living quarters, but only got as far as the side of the front desk before he stopped and turned. Millie knew this was when the deputy sheriff confronted him. "What do you want?" he said with a scowl. Millie saw his frustration. He was agitated about his wife. "You know I ain't no outlaw and I ain't going anywhere till I check on Samantha." He paused again, a snarl on his face. "This?" He reached up. That's when he was shot. He flew backwards and disappeared.

It was alarming to witness the scene again and to be close enough to hear what he was saying. She stood frozen a moment, stunned to silence, wishing she could wake him from his trance and ask him directly for information.

However, Emerson was right—the deputy knew he wasn't Bronco Bill, and he knew Emerson wasn't going for his gun.

In order to see what, if anything, was in the grandfather clock, the lights needed to be on. She strode to the switch and illuminated the parlor, then walked to it. There was a knob at the bottom. Millie had always assumed it was decorative. She tugged at it and a small drawer opened. Two keys were inside, one for the clock, and another one. She picked up the extra key and turned it over in her hand.

"Emerson, you are one smart dude," she said. Either that or he was super cautious, and rightfully so. Imitating Emerson's actions, Millie took the key behind the front desk. All the drawers on her right had been damaged. The front desk drawer had sustained damage though it still opened, but she had assumed the smaller drawer on the top left was either stuck or decorative. It was always too dark to see much of anything, but now she knew to look for a keyhole. She ran upstairs, grabbed her flashlight and hurried back to the desk area.

The drawer in question had barely missed Kenny's sledgehammer. Millie felt around and discovered a small keyhole under the desk in the chair cubby and shined her light on it. She put the key in and turned. The drawer popped open about an inch. Pulling it open the rest of the way, she felt around. In the back was a small box. Millie lifted it out and examined it. It was light and wrapped in antique Christmas paper. Millie's shoulders sagged. The box and the drawer were both too small to hold treasure. Maybe there really and truly wasn't any.

But after Emerson had disappeared behind the counter, he had done something else. "The wall." She stood and pressed against several panels. Nothing happened. "Agh! What are you trying to show me, Emerson?" Millie went back to the small drawer and felt around the sides, then she felt in the cubby below. A knob, at the very back on the inside left. Her heart drummed with the excitement of discovery as she started to slide it, hoping to release some type of panel-safe. But then she hesitated. As the great-great descendant of Emerson and Samantha Ballard, Lonny should get the honors.

Itching with curiosity and impatient for Lonny's return, she put everything back the way it was, turned the lights off, and headed upstairs to her bedroom to read; there was no way she could sleep. As she got to the upstairs landing, however, a light flashed across the window that faced the barn. It was late. Without turning on the upstairs light, she went to the window. The mountains were merely a silhouette against an indigo sky, and graced by millions of stars. "This is a great view, Emerson." For all its glamor and hype, Phoenix didn't have a night view remotely this remarkable.

Light glowed from slats in the barn and illuminated a county sheriff's vehicle. It was Len. Sure it was Christmas Eve, and sure he was at work, but she needed to know his motive for traipsing her around town and for the rumors. Who did stuff like that, and why? So, although Millie had already said her goodbyes to him, she headed down the stairs with her flashlight.

Twenty-Seven

When Millie got about halfway to the barn, she hesitated, taking in the situation. The light from the barn exposed a large number of parked trucks. The one closest in her vision was Len's work vehicle. Nerves fluttered in her chest and she chewed a fingernail. If she went back to the hotel and waited, maybe Lonny would be back soon and go out there with her. But the idea of being used for some warped motive of Len's, the fact that she had fallen for his scheme, and the idea that the townspeople kept bugging Lonny, made her angry. Shining her flashlight in front of her, she took another step, her feet crunching on the dry ground.

A whoosh of cold air circled around her like a dust devil, as if trying to push her toward the hotel. "M-i-l-l-i-e," Emerson whispered. "D-o-n'-t g-o."

"Stay with me," she said. "I need to speak with Deputy Begay." She could wait by his truck until he got done dealing with the teens.

As Millie neared the barn, shouts grew more noticeable. The noise continued and sounded like a brawl, but he would have the teens kicked out soon enough. Determination propelled her forward to a safe distance from the door—near Len's vehicle. Once at the door, she caught her breath and felt little beads of sweat tickling at her hairline. She saw dozens of lustful, excited faces. Adults, not teens, sitting on bales of straw with fists of money in their hands and either rifles or pistols on their laps. Two roosters fought in the center of the barn, silver blades glistening from their legs. A couple of dead or maimed and bloody roosters lay limp in the straw.

Chill dread, like an icicle, etched up her spine—she needed to get out of there! It was a cockfight, just like in Emerson's day. And Deputy Begay wasn't arresting them—he was gambling with them. This was why he'd spread rumors about dangerous activities at the barn—to scare the locals into staying away, and to scare her. Her heart pounded. She turned, her heel crunching the dirt. She would run to the hotel, get her keys, and get out of there.

"Hey, who is that?" someone shouted.

"I bet it's Millie Crump. Go get control of the situation," Deputy Begay growled. "It's a felony charge and possible jail time if the boss finds out."

Now she more fully understood the rumors and all of Deputy Begay's attention. She wasn't someone Len was interested in—she was a *situation* needing to be controlled so he could continue his illegal activity. Millie scanned her surroundings, trying to quickly form a plan. It was too far to the hotel. The men would outrun her, and who knew what would happen then?

Millie zigged to her right and ducked behind a bush, dropping to her knees just as three men rushed from the barn with rifles in hand. "Let's spread out," one of them said. "We'll find 'er faster that way." They strode toward the hotel, each taking a different route.

A cold breeze swirled around her, urging her to move. "I'm safer here," she whispered. But the breeze swirled more insistently. "Okay, okay." Crouching like an old woman, she scampered past the trucks, stumbling into a shin dagger agave and cutting her arm. She kept going. Reaching the boulders at the mountain's base, Millie crawled up and around the rocks, worrying faintly about stepping in a rattlesnake den. From this slightly higher elevation, she saw through the open door that the cockfight was still going on. A coyote howled from a distance. Millie froze, hoping it was a far distance. A waning moon revealed silhouettes of the three others forming a wide arch. They poked in bushes and called to one another.

Deputy Begay came out. "Millie, you're safe. There's no need to hide." He walked around his vehicle.

Truck lights pulled off the highway and into the hotel's circular drive. It was Lonny! He got out of his truck and went inside the hotel. Relief twitched at her lips and she started down the mountain. But as she neared the parked trucks by the barn, Millie drew in a gasp, realizing he could be caught in a deadly situation. Anxiety riddled through her. He would be in danger if he came out to the barn looking for her, and Millie couldn't get to the hotel without the deputy seeing her.

But rather than look for her, Lonny left the hotel, ran back to his truck and drove away.

What? She wasn't even worth looking for? Millie's shoulders slumped, her knees buckling. She'd been kidding herself, loving him again and wishing they were a couple. Lonny's only interest in her was their shared history of the hotel. She took a few breaths and blinked back the thought. *That's Mother talking.* She gulped hard at that reality. She had become cynical, like her mother. It would be hard to change, to give everyone the benefit of the doubt, but she had to try. Lonny would be back, and she would survive.

Deputy Begay moved away from his truck and into the shadows. "Millie, this is all a misunderstanding," he called.

"My roosters are champions. They're beautiful. Come and watch. It isn't animal cruelty when this is what they live for." He batted at some brush, getting closer to her.

She crouched behind a creosote bush. Her teeth chattered and a cold breeze from the mountain forced Millie to pull her faux suede Chyla drape tighter. She used to love her "jacket," but now it clung to her like cheap tinsel reminding her that her life had been as shallow.

Millie rubbed her aching knees with the stark realization that she couldn't wait for Lonny's rescue much longer; she'd catch pneumonia or freeze. But she didn't need anyone to rescue her—she had always done perfectly well on her own. When Len looked away, she pushed herself up, stretched her legs, and stood. It was a long way to the hotel, and it was a long way to the highway. But if she stayed in the brush, maybe she could make it. It was dark. Len probably wouldn't see her.

Before settling on a course of action, Len lunged out of the dark and grabbed her. "Let me go!" she screamed.

"Now darlin' that's no way to treat your old high school friend."

"We weren't friends in high school." Millie kicked at him, but missed.

"No, but we should have been. We have a lot in common, you and I," he cooed in her ear.

"Not in the things that count," Millie countered. Just because their fathers had abandoned them both didn't mean they were alike in any other way.

"Now I need you to see the situation from my side. I don't want to lose my job over this—and I can't see jail time. You know that as a sheriff's deputy I wouldn't last long behind bars. I've done a lot of good in this community, helped put away a lot of criminals." He pulled her toward the barn as she struggled against him. "Consider the consequences of your actions. Ya know if we can't see eye to eye on this thing, I'm going to need to tell Lonny about our secret kisses, and of our satisfying interlude at my home."

He really was a letch. Millie shuddered. "You know nothing happened. I never kissed you, and I've never been to your house."

Deputy Begay grinned sardonically. "He doesn't know it, though. It'll put a wedge of doubt between you—and right when things were looking up. It would probably kill Mr. Medina to hear such things."

Millie trembled at his words. Len was right, hearing such nonsense would be hard on the Medinas. She straightened her shoulders and took a couple of steps with the deputy.

"I knew you'd see it my way."

"Of course," she said, but the moment he loosened his grip, she kneed him in the groin, struck him with the flashlight, and pulled away.

"She's over here!" He groaned and fell to the ground.

There was too much open space between the barn and the hotel, and the other three men were out there. She would also have to run past the open barn door to get to the hotel. It was too dangerous. So, using the shadows cast by trees and the mountain, Millie rushed back toward the mountain, stepping behind a large boulder to catch her breath.

The three men searching to the south and east ran back toward Deputy Begay. Although Millie was hidden behind the boulder, they ran toward her. With each step the men took, Millie fought the urge to bolt, but they would see her if she moved.

"Guys, come over here," Len shouted. "Spread out. She's headed toward the mountain."

Millie started to move—she itched to move—but her best chance to remain unseen was to hold perfectly still.

A rush of wind blew down the mountain, bringing with it flakes of snow.

Deputy Begay pulled himself up and shouted, "The Sheriff's been dispatched! Get rid of the evidence and let's get out of here!"

The three men turned from the mountain and hurried into the barn, joining the others who had stayed. They kicked dead and maimed roosters into the pit.

Deputy Begay stared toward her. "I know you're there, Millie. It doesn't need to end like this." His voice sounded friendly as he stepped closer. "I don't want to hurt you, but I don't want you to hurt me, either. Can't you see I want us to be friends?"

Millie's heart thudded, her breathing shallow. He was trying to bait her into saying something and giving away her location. She bent down, knees on the boulder before her, and hand-over-hand, crawled from rock to rock and down the mountainside. She stood to make a run for it, and at that exact moment, she heard a sound in the shrubs. Deputy Begay grabbed her. She screamed!

"You weren't worth all the time I wasted on you," the deputy snarled. "Don't even think of moving or telling the Sheriff about this. You'll regret it if you do." He pulled her down to his vehicle and shoved her inside, jumping in beside her. He turned on the engine and crept around to the back of the barn with his lights off.

Millie couldn't understand what he was doing. "Being caught with gaming roosters isn't as serious as kidnapping. You should let me go."

Len clenched his jaw and shook his head, staring forward. "I never wanted it to end like this—I care about you, Millie. I always have." He hung his head and sighed. "Just go."

Without a word, she scooted over and stepped out of his vehicle while keeping an eye on the deputy to make sure he didn't change his mind. She hurried toward the mountain to hide again, crouching between the boulders and hoping Deputy Begay didn't come back for her. To her right, there was shouting and confusion as the others all scattered toward their vehicles. The sounds of their slamming doors reverberating in the night.

Sirens blared, getting closer. Flashing lights of the county vehicles appeared. She ducked behind another boulder in anticipation of their headlights, but the group from the barn backed away with their lights off. They all but disappeared in a cloud of dust as they raced toward the hotel to get to the highway.

Police cars and sheriff SUVs charged onto the property, blocking any escape by the highway. Some of them abandoned their vehicles and ran into the darkness. A few officers chased after them. The sheriff and other deputies' vehicles surrounded the trucks. Other officials came out, weapons drawn, and used their vehicles for cover. The sheriff got out of his vehicle, and standing behind his truck door, called through a megaphone for their surrender.

Twenty-Eight

Millie shivered, her teeth chattering as the snow continued falling. *What will I do, wait here and freeze to death?* She didn't dare move until Len Begay and the others were apprehended. There was only One she could turn to this Christmas Eve. "Dear Lord," she prayed, "please bless me to survive this mess and help me to overcome my past."

After whispering her prayer, Millie waited, still afraid to move. One by one, the sheriff and his deputies apprehended the others. Deputy Begay drove around the barn, jumped out, and pretended he was one of the arresting officers. But after his protests and making several attempts to escape, the sheriff cuffed him as well. All his interest in her and in the hotel had been merely for his own gain.

The snow flitted to a stop, but Millie's teeth chattered, and she emitted short puffs of icy air. She rubbed her frozen hands across her arms, hoping the friction would warm her. Sheriff Adams went inside the barn. She watched, unsure whether it was safe to come out. Lonny drove toward the barn then, and Millie wouldn't stay on the mountain longer. It was safe. She was safe.

"Millie!" Lonny called.

"I'm here!" she answered, but the wind blew her voice away.

Lonny went inside the barn, still shouting for her.

She sat on a boulder, bent down and picked up her flashlight, then shined it in front of her so she could get onto flat ground.

Her heart pounded as she stepped carefully over the rocks, taking more time than she wanted to, trembling from the cold and from the night's unsettling events. When she finally reached flat land, shining her flashlight as she went, she looked for signs of danger. Something nearby growled. The hairs on her head tingled. Millie pointed her flashlight beam around her in an arc, illuminating several coyotes stalking their way from the mountain and toward the open barn door.

Her heart lurched into her throat. She walked backward while keeping an eye on the animals. When she got past the barn, she turned and raced toward safety, then glanced back to make sure the coyotes weren't following, and ran into something solid. She screamed.

Lonny's arms wrapped around her. "It's okay. You're safe now."

Millie clung to him and wept. "I was so afraid," she said, shaking uncontrollably.

Lonny supported Millie as they walked to the hotel, repeatedly reassuring her in calm tones that she was safe. He barely believed it himself and couldn't hold her tight enough. He'd almost lost her, but he had felt a prompting to come. "Thank you, *Abuelo*," he whispered into her hair.

"I thought they were going to find me—they did find me," she said. "I, I was alone."

She still verged on hysterical, but Lonny couldn't hold in his feelings one moment longer. He had almost lost her and he had to do everything in his power to keep that from ever happening again. He stopped just inside the hotel entry, lifting her chin with his fingers. "You never have to be alone again if you don't want to be." He searched her expression.

"What do you mean?" She took in a shaky breath.

"I mean, you scared me half to death," he said in a scolding tone. "When I came back to the hotel and your car was there, but you weren't." He shook his head. "I saw the lights and heard the commotion, and knew you'd gone out to the barn. I wanted to charge in there and demand your safety." He grinned crookedly. "But I decided a call for help would ensure your safety more than my trying to play hero." He held her tight, not wanting to let go.

Millie hid her face in his shirt as though she was embarrassed. He lifted her chin again and gazed into her eyes, and whispered, "I don't want to ever let you go again."

She turned her head questioningly. He saw she was still too stunned from her ordeal, but he couldn't tuck away his emotions and pretend he hadn't said anything. He needed her to know, tonight, how he felt. There might not be a tomorrow.

"Millie Crump, I was too young to stop you from moving out of my life fourteen years ago, but I'm not now. I'm an old-fashioned guy and I don't want to pretend. You know I don't have much money, but I'll make up for it with the abundance of love I feel for you. We can have a long engagement, if you'd like, but eventually I've just got to call you mine." He gazed into her eyes, searching for any sign that she felt the same. His shoulders slumped. That was not a look of joy on her face. He should have waited.

It sounded as though Lonny wanted to marry her. Millie must have hit her head, or maybe she was in shock.

They'd only been together a week. She touched her torn sweater and the gash on her arm, momentarily distracted.

"Well, will you marry me?" His voice sounded impatient, his eyes revealed hurt.

"I've never really loved anyone else," she murmured. "But why would you want to marry me?" She had done nothing but doubt him.

"I love you, that's why." Lonny leaned forward tentatively; she met him part way, and his lips touched hers. They were warm and soft. His arms wrapped around her. Pulling her in, he kissed her again, revealing the feelings of his heart.

This was better than a Christmas miracle—or rather, it was a miracle meant just for her. "I will marry you, Alonzo Medina," Millie said breathlessly.

"And I will marry you, Millie Crump." He leaned in to kiss her again, but she put her fingers to his mouth.

"I have a discovery for you to make." She took his hand and walked with him to the lobby.

Lonny pulled against her. "Hey, I tell you I'm an old-fashioned guy, and already you're tempting me?" He grinned, indicating the stairs with a nod.

Millie's cheeks heated. "It's not that." She took him to the grandfather clock and pulled the key from the drawer, handing it to him. "I found it this evening."

He turned it around in his fingers. "What's it for?"

Millie smiled. "I'll show you." She took his hand and walked him behind the front counter. "There's a keyhole under here," she said, shining her flashlight underneath. "Go ahead—it'll open the drawer."

Lonny got down on the floor and turned the key. The skinny drawer popped open about an inch. He looked at her. "What's this?" A smile crept over his face.

"That's an almost empty drawer." Millie reached inside. "I think this is Emerson's last Christmas gift to Samantha."

She pulled the box out and set it on the counter.

"I guess there's no need to wait until Christmas to see what it is." He reached for the present.

Pressing her hand over his, Millie stopped him. "I think that you'll be able to open a secret compartment if you push the knob right here." She put his fingers over the knob on the inside of the cubby. He pushed it while looking for movement. "Nothing happened."

"Maybe you have to push against this panel." She indicated the wall with a touch.

Lonny stood and applied pressure to the panel. "I think there could be a wall safe or something," he said. "It seems to want to open." Using both hands, he applied pressure to both sides of the panel at the same time. It moved slightly. Lonny took hold of the edges and pulled. "It's stuck." He pulled and tugged and got it to open several inches. Millie shined her flashlight inside.

"Look at that." The safe was crammed full of stacks of dusty bills, gold coins, and a pile of silver dollars—her Christmas wish for the Medinas. "You'll be able to make repairs to the Ballard hotel after all."

Lonny stared open-mouthed at the drawer. "I bet that most of this belongs to the bank that Bronco Bill stole it from."

"Probably. But I also bet they've offered a reward for its return." She was pleased for the Medinas, but was finding the treasure enough to help Emerson Ballard rest in peace—would he care that Lonny had claimed the hotel as his heir? Millie glanced around, but Emerson was as silent as Lonny.

"What do you think?" She tilted her head, trying to discern his mood. "If there's enough, will you repair the hotel?"

Lonny nodded. "It's surreal. I grew up with this hotel, with you. Even though I kept having these feelings, I hadn't wanted to believe we were heirs because I felt this property that meant so much to me, and to us, was out of my reach financially." Lonny wiped his hands over his face. "I'm barely starting to believe even now. I really am an heir, and Emerson Alonzo Ballard really was my great-great-grandfather."

He said it with the same awe that Millie had felt all week. "Now open the box." Millie picked it up and handed it to him. "Let's see what's inside." Maybe it was more treasure.

He peeled off the brittle paper wrapping and opened the box. Inside was a small, yellowing piece of paper. It was handwritten, and said, "My dearest Samantha, my wish this Christmas and for all time, is that our hotel will stand as a testament of my love for you. And that one hundred years from now, if the hotel is still standing, our great-great-grandchildren will want to continue our legacy." Under the note was an exquisitely detailed nativity set made of porcelain.

Lonny caressed Millie's cheek. "My Christmas wish this year was you," he murmured. "Millie, I promise to love you as much, or more, than Emerson loved Samantha."

Millie twined her arm with Lonny's. "They'll write stories about us," she said. "Because our love is so true that it has already withstood fourteen years of separation. It'll last for another hundred and fourteen."

Lonny leaned forward, touching his lips to hers, and kissed her tenderly. Millie put her hand to his neck, drawing him closer into what felt like a moment of pure bliss.

When Lonny pulled away, he asked, "Do you think Emerson really wants me in his hotel?" He glanced worriedly around. "We haven't seen him." He looked at the nativity, then pulled a porcelain piece from the box. "This is perfect for the front counter once it's renovated." He took the other pieces from the box and placed them on the desk. "I'm going to have his Christmas card preserved and framed. I'll hang it on the wall along with their picture, so everyone who enters can see."

"Emerson and Samantha would both be proud to have you taking care of their hotel." As she spoke, a chilly gust swirled around her and Lonny. "It's him," she said. He appeared before them in a translucent version of his human form. Millie noted how happy he looked.

"I will care for the hotel, and I will make you proud," Lonny said. "Merry Christmas, *Abuelo*, Grandfather."

Emerson tipped his hat.

"*Buenos noches*, good night." Millie inhaled deeply, feeling a sense of great joy. "Rest in peace, Emerson Alonzo Ballard, and Merry Christmas." The Christmas ghost swirled around them one more time and then breezed out and through the door.

This year, each of them had gotten their Christmas wish.

Author Notes

I had a lot of fun researching Arizona history for this story. I hope you enjoy it. Some readers like to know how much of a story is real. Is it all part of the author's imagination or is it based on the truth?

Although used fictitiously, Solomon, Arizona is a real town in Graham County, Arizona, in an area known as the Gila Valley, which encompasses Safford, Thatcher, Central, and Pima, among other small communities.

Solomonville, originally known as Pueblo Viejo, was founded by Isadore and Anna Solomon. They were immigrants from Poland. Pueblo Viejo was renamed Solomonville by the mail carrier. The Solomons were very industrious and started many business ventures in the area, including the Solomon Hotel, a two-story wooden structure with a wrap-around porch. More about Isadore and Anna Solomon can be found here: http://www.jmaw. org/isadore-anna-solomon-arizona/

The fictional adobe hotel that I have described was based on pictures of Schieffelin Hall in Tombstone, Arizona.

Bronco Bill was a real bank robber whose claim to fame is the purported lost treasure near Solomonville, Arizona. It is said that after he was released from jail, he never returned to Solomonville. More about Bronco Bill can be found here:
https://www.legendsofamerica.com/bronco-bill-loses- against-wells-fargo/

To learn more about Arizona's long history of cockfighting, you may search this website:
https://www.washingtonpost.com/archive/politics/1998/12/27/in-arizona-tradition-of-cockfighting-comes-to-a-close/87e50722-e379-420b-900a-dee0f7d7ff21/?utm_term=.2ee9d90aa95d

Las Posadas is a Christmas tradition that has deep roots in the Mexican culture. You may learn more about this annual tradition here: https://www.franciscanmedia.org/las-posadas-a- mexican-christmas-tradition/

About the Author

For much of Mrs. Scott's childhood, she could be found nestled against a branch high in a pecan tree, and reading a book. A series of spy novels may yet be written about her antics while camouflaged within those branches.

Her favorite reads as a youth were fantasy and mystery, and it delighted Tina when her mother read to her from Grimm's Fairy Tales and the stories of Hans Christian Andersen. Her current favorites include historical and contemporary romance, fantasy, and cozy mysteries.

Tina and her husband have seven children and a growing number of grandchildren. Other than large family get-togethers involving lots of food and fun, she enjoys writing, watercolor painting, long walks, ice cream, and traveling to Europe—especially to her father's ancestral home of Denmark.

Connect with Tina on social media:
http://www.facebook.com/TinasWritingAdventure/
https://www.instagram.com/tinapetersonscott/
www.linkedin.com/in/tinapetersonscott

Other Novels by Tina Scott

Farewell, My Denmark – Tina Peterson Scott
My Sweet Danish Rose – Tina Peterson Scott
Menopausal fairy Mischief – Tina Scott

I would be honored if you would review Millie's Christmas Spirit on Amazon, Barnes & Noble, and Goodreads. Thank you, Tina Scott

www.ingramcontent.com/pod-product-compliance
Lightning Source LLC
Chambersburg PA
CBHW070300120726
47910CB00007B/2317